*His eyes were bold on her body,
as if he knew exactly what was
under her clothing.*

The thought of Callaghan Hart's mouth on her lips made Tess's breath catch in her throat.

She'd always been a little afraid of her big, brooding boss. But lately at night she lay wondering how it would feel if he kissed her. She'd thought about it a *lot,* to her shame.

Callaghan was mature, experienced, confident— all the things Tess wasn't. She knew she couldn't handle an affair with him. She was equally sure he wouldn't have any amorous interest in a novice like her.

She'd *been* sure, Tess amended.

Because Callaghan was looking at her now in a way he'd never looked at her before....

Dear Reader,

March roars in like a lion at Silhouette Romance, starting with popular author Susan Meier and *Husband from 9 to 5*, her exciting contribution to LOVING THE BOSS, a six-book series in which office romance leads to happily-ever-after. In this sparkling story, a bump on the head has a boss-loving woman believing she's married to the man of her dreams....

In March 1998, beloved author Diana Palmer launched VIRGIN BRIDES. This month, *Callaghan's Bride* not only marks the anniversary of this special Romance promotion, but it continues her wildly successful LONG, TALL TEXANS series! As a rule, hard-edged, hard-bodied Callaghan Hart distrusted sweet, virginal, starry-eyed young ladies. But ranch cook Tess Brady had this cowboy hankerin' to break all his rules.

Judy Christenberry's LUCKY CHARM SISTERS miniseries resumes with a warm, emotional pretend engagement story that might just lead to *A Ring for Cinderella*. When a jaded attorney delivers a very pregnant stranger's baby, he starts a journey toward healing...and making this woman his *Texas Bride*, the heartwarming new novel by Kate Thomas. In *Soldier and the Society Girl* by Vivian Leiber, the month's HE'S MY HERO selection, sparks fly when a true-blue, true-grit American hero requires the protocol services of a refined blue blood. A lone-wolf lawman meets his match in an indomitable schoolteacher— and her moonshining granny—in Gayle Kaye's *Sheriff Takes a Bride*, part of FAMILY MATTERS.

Enjoy this month's fantastic offerings, and make sure to return each and every month to Silhouette Romance!

Mary-Theresa Hussey

Mary-Theresa Hussey
Senior Editor, Silhouette Romance

Please address questions and book requests to:
Silhouette Reader Service
U.S.: 3010 Walden Ave., P.O. Box 1325, Buffalo, NY 14269
Canadian: P.O. Box 609, Fort Erie, Ont. L2A 5X3

VIRGIN BRIDES

CALLAGHAN'S BRIDE

DIANA PALMER

Silhouette
R O M A N C E™
Published by Silhouette Books
America's Publisher of Contemporary Romance

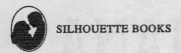 SILHOUETTE BOOKS

ISBN 0-373-19355-6

CALLAGHAN'S BRIDE

This edition published by arrangement with Harlequin Books S.A.

® and TM are trademarks of Harlequin Books S.A., used under license. Trademarks indicated with ® are registered in the United States Patent and Trademark Office, the Canadian Trade Marks Office and in other countries.

Printed in U.S.A.

Dear Reader,

It was a privilege for me to participate in the
VIRGIN BRIDES series for Silhouette Romance.
Marriage is the greatest adventure of all, and to embark
upon it with innocence is almost an act of bravery these
days. As our society has grown in technology and
sophistication, it seems to me that we have sacrificed
idealism somewhere along the way. This should not be.
Virtue, purity, honor, self-sacrifice and duty are beautiful,
enduring ideals. They make life worthwhile; they give us
a purpose, a place in the world regardless of our social or
financial standing. They define us as individuals and give
us higher goals to strive for. They illuminate us
spiritually.

One of my favorite characters in fiction is Don Quixote,
who struggled in his endearing way to restore honor and
morality to a tarnished, weary world. I have always tried
to emphasize these virtues in what I write. The
VIRGIN BRIDES series brings idealism as well as
romantic magic to the Silhouette Romance line, and I am
proud to participate in it. Happy Anniversary to the
VIRGIN BRIDES. Long may they endure.

Love,

Diana Palmer

Chapter One

The kitchen cat twirled around Tess's legs and almost tripped her on her way to the oven. She smiled at it ruefully and made time to pour it a bowl of cat food. The cat was always hungry, it seemed. Probably it was still afraid of starving, because it had been a stray when Tess took it in.

It was the bane of Tess Brady's existence that she couldn't resist stray or hurt animals. Most of her young life had been spent around rodeos with her father, twice the world champion calf roper. She hadn't had a lot to do with animals, which might have explained why she loved them. Now that her father was gone, and she was truly on her own, she enjoyed having little things to take care of. Her charges ranged from birds with broken wings to sick calves. There was an unbroken procession.

This cat was her latest acquisition. It had come to the back door as a kitten just after Thanksgiving, squalling in the dark, rainy night. Tess had taken it in, despite the grumbling from two of her three bosses. The big boss, the one who didn't like her, had been her only ally in letting the cat stay.

That surprised her. Callaghan Hart was one tough hombre. He'd been a captain in the Green Berets and had seen action in Operation Desert Storm. He was the next-to-eldest of the five Hart brothers who owned the sweeping Hart Ranch Properties, a conglomerate of ranches and feedlots located in several western states. The headquarter ranch was in Jacobsville, Texas. Simon, the eldest brother, was an attorney in San Antonio. Corrigan, who was four years younger than Simon, had married over a year and a half ago. He and his wife Dorie had a new baby son. There were three other Hart bachelors left in Jacobsville: Reynard, the youngest, Leopold, the second youngest, and Callaghan who was just two years younger than Simon. They all lived on the Jacobsville property.

Tess's father had worked for the Hart brothers for a little over six months when he dropped dead in the corral of a heart attack. It had been devastating for Tess, whose mother had run out on them when she was little. Cray Brady, her father, was an only child. There wasn't any other family that she knew of. The Harts had also known that. When their housekeeper had expressed a desire to retire, Tess had seemed the perfect replacement because she could cook and keep house. She could also ride like a cowboy and shoot like an expert and curse in fluent Spanish, but the Hart boys didn't know about those skills because she'd never had occasion to display them. Her talents these days were confined to making the fluffy biscuits the brothers couldn't live without and producing basic but hearty meals. Everything except sweets because none of the brothers seemed to like them.

It would have been the perfect job, even with Leopold's

endless pranks, except that she was afraid of Callaghan. It showed, which made things even worse.

He watched her all the time, from her curly red-gold hair and pale blue eyes to her small feet, as if he was just waiting for her to make a mistake so that he could fire her. Over breakfast, those black Spanish eyes would cut into her averted face like a diamond. They were set in a lean, dark face with a broad forehead and a heavy, jutting brow. He had a big nose and big ears and big feet, but his long, chiseled mouth was perfect and he had thick, straight hair as black as a raven. He wasn't handsome, but he was commanding and arrogant and frightening even to other men. Leopold had once told her that the brothers tried to step in if Cag ever lost his temper enough to get physical. He had an extensive background in combat, but even his size alone made him dangerous. It was fortunate that he rarely let his temper get the best of him.

Tess had never been able to understand why Cag disliked her so much. He hadn't said a word of protest when the others decided to offer her the job of housekeeper and cook after her father's sudden death. And he was the one who made Leopold apologize after a particularly unpleasant prank at a party. But he never stopped cutting at Tess or finding ways to get at her.

Like this morning. She'd always put strawberry preserves on the table for breakfast, because the brothers preferred them. But this morning Cag had wanted apple butter and she couldn't find any. He'd been scathing about her lack of organization and stomped off without a second biscuit or another cup of coffee.

"His birthday is a week from Saturday," Leopold had explained ruefully. "He hates getting older."

Reynard agreed. "Last year, he went away for a week

around this time of the year. Nobody knew where he was, either.'' He shook his head. ''Poor old Cag.''

''Why do you call him that?'' Tess asked curiously.

''I don't know,'' Rey said, smiling thoughtfully. ''I guess because, of all of us, he's the most alone.''

She hadn't thought of it that way, but Rey was right. Cag was alone. He didn't date, and he didn't go out ''with the boys,'' as many other men did. He kept to himself. When he wasn't working—which was rarely—he was reading history books. It had surprised Tess during her first weeks as housekeeper to find that he read Spanish colonial history, in Spanish. She hadn't known that he was bilingual, although she found it out later when two of the Hispanic cowboys got into a no-holds-barred fight with a Texas cowboy who'd been deliberately baiting them. The Texas cowboy had been fired and the two Latinos had been quietly and efficiently cursed within an inch of their lives in the coldest, most bitingly perfect Spanish Tess had ever heard. She herself was bilingual, having spent most of her youth in the Southwest.

Cag didn't know she spoke Spanish. It was one of many accomplishments she was too shy to share with him. She kept to herself most of the time, except when Dorie came with Corrigan to the ranch to visit. They lived in a house of their own several miles away—although it was still on the Hart ranch. Dorie was sweet and kind, and Tess adored her. Now that the baby was here, Tess looked forward to the visits even more. She adored children.

What she didn't adore was Herman. Although she was truly an animal lover, her affection didn't extend to snakes. The great albino python with his yellow-patterned white skin and red eyes terrified her. He lived in an enormous aquarium against one wall of Cag's room, and he had a nasty habit of escaping. Tess had found him in a variety of unlikely spots, including the washing machine. He wasn't dangerous because Cag kept him well-fed, and he was always closely watched for a day or so after he ate— which wasn't very often. Eventually she learned not to scream. Like measles and colds, Herman was a force of nature that simply had to be accepted. Cag loved the vile reptile. It seemed to be the only thing that he really cared about.

Well, maybe he liked the cat, too. She'd seen him playing with it once, with a long piece of string. He didn't know that. When he wasn't aware anyone was watching, he seemed to be a different person. And nobody had forgotten about what happened after he saw what was subsequently referred to as the "pig" movie. Rey had sworn that his older brother was all but in tears during one of the scenes in the touching, funny motion picture. Cag saw it three times in the theater and later bought a copy of his own.

Since the movie, Cag didn't eat pork anymore, not ham nor sausage nor bacon. And he made everyone who did feel uncomfortable. It was one of many paradoxes about this complicated man. He wasn't afraid of anything on this earth, but apparently he had a soft heart hidden deep inside. Tess had never been privileged to see it, because Cag didn't like her. She wished that she wasn't so uneasy around him. But then, most people were.

Christmas Eve came later in the week, and Tess served an evening meal fit for royalty, complete with all the trimmings. The married Harts were starting their own tradition for Christmas Day, so the family celebration was on Christmas Eve.

Tess ate with them, because all four brothers had looked outraged when she started to set a place for herself in the kitchen with widowed Mrs. Lewis, who came almost every day to do the mopping and waxing and general cleaning that Tess didn't have time for. It was very democratic of them, she supposed, and it did feel nice to at least appear to be part of a family—even if it wasn't her own. Mrs. Lewis went home to her visiting children, anyway, so Tess would have been in the kitchen alone.

She was wearing the best dress she had—a nice red plaid one, but it was cheap and it looked it when compared to the dress that Dorie Hart was wearing. They went out of their way to make her feel secure, though, and by the time they started on the pumpkin and pecan pies and the huge dark fruitcake, she wasn't worried about her dress anymore. Everyone included her in the conversation. Except for Cag's silence, it would have been perfect. But he didn't even look at her. She tried not to care.

She got presents, another unexpected treat, in return for her homemade gifts. She'd crocheted elegant trim for two pillowcases that she'd embroidered for the Harts, matching them to the color schemes in their individual bedrooms— something she'd asked Dorie to conspire with her about. She did elegant crochet work. She was making things for Dorie's baby boy in her spare time, a labor of love.

The gifts she received weren't handmade, but she loved them just the same. The brothers chipped in to buy her a winter coat. It was a black leather one with big cuffs and a sash. She'd never seen anything so beautiful in all her life, and she cried over it. The women gave her presents, too. She had a delicious floral perfume from Dorie and a designer scarf in just the right shades of blue from Mrs. Lewis. She felt on top of the world as she cleared away the dinner dishes and got to work in the kitchen.

Leo paused by the counter and tugged at her apron strings with a mischievous grin.

"Don't you dare," she warned him. She smiled, though, before she turned her attention back to the dishes.

"Cag didn't say a word," he remarked. "He's gone off to ride the fence line near the river with Mack before it gets dark." Mack was the cattle foreman, a man even more silent than Cag. The ranch was so big that there were foremen over every aspect of it: the cattle, the horses, the mechanical crew, the office crew, the salesmen—there was even a veterinarian on retainer. Tess's father had been the livestock foreman for the brief time he spent at the Hart ranch before his untimely death. Tess's mother had left them when Tess was still a little girl, sick of the nomadic life that her husband loved. In recent years Tess hadn't heard a word from her. She was glad. She hoped she never had to see her mother again.

"Oh." She put a plate in the dishwasher. "Because of me?" she added quietly.

He hesitated. "I don't know." He toyed with a knife on the counter. "He hasn't been himself lately. Well," he amended with a wry smile, "he has, but he's been worse than usual."

"I haven't done anything, have I?" she asked, and turned worried eyes up to his.

She was so young, he mused, watching all the uncertainties rush across her smooth, lightly freckled face. She wasn't pretty, but she wasn't plain, either. She had an inner light that seemed to radiate from her when she was happy. He liked hearing her sing when she mopped and swept, when she went out to feed the few chickens they kept for egg production. Despite the fairly recent tragedy in her life, she was a happy person.

"No," he said belatedly. "You haven't done a thing. You'll get used to Cag's moods. He doesn't have them too often. Just at Christmas, his birthday and sometimes in the summer.''

"Why?'' she asked.

He hesitated, then shrugged. "He went overseas in Operation Desert Storm,'' he said. "He never talks about it. Whatever he did was classified. But he was in some tight corners and he came home wounded. While he was recuperating in West Germany, his fiancée married somebody else. Christmas and July remind him, and he gets broody.''

She grimaced. "He doesn't seem the sort of man who would ask a woman to marry him unless he was serious.''

"He isn't. It hurt him, really bad. He hasn't had much time for women since.'' He smiled gently. "It gets sort of funny when we go to conventions. There's Cag in black tie, standing out like a beacon, and women just follow him around like pet calves. He never seems to notice.''

"I guess he's still healing,'' she said, and relaxed a little. At least it wasn't just her that set him off.

"I don't know that he ever will,'' he replied. He pursed his lips, watching her work. "You're very domestic, aren't you?''

She poured detergent into the dishwasher with a smile and turned it on. "I've always had to be. My mother left us when I was little, although she came back to visit just once, when I was sixteen. We never saw her again.'' She shivered inwardly at the memory. "Anyway, I learned to cook and clean for Daddy at an early age.''

"No brothers or sisters?''

She shook her head. "Just us. I wanted to get a job or go on to college after high school, to help out. But he needed me, and I just kept putting it off. I'm glad I did, now.'' Her eyes clouded a little. "I loved him to death. I kept thinking though, what if we'd known about his heart in time, could anything have been done?''

"You can't do that to yourself," he stated. "Things happen. Bad things, sometimes. You have to realize that you can't control life."

"That's a hard lesson."

He nodded. "But it's one we all have to learn." He frowned slightly. "Just how old are you—twenty or so?"

She looked taken aback. "I'm twenty-one. I'll be twenty-two in March."

Now he looked taken aback. "You don't seem that old."

She chuckled. "Is that a compliment or an insult?"

He cocked an amused eyebrow. "I suppose you'll see it as the latter."

She wiped an imaginary spot on the counter with a cloth. "Callaghan's the oldest, isn't he?"

"Simon," he corrected. "Cag's going to be thirty-eight on Saturday."

She averted her eyes, as if she didn't want him to see whatever was in them. "He took a long time to get engaged."

"Herman doesn't exactly make for lasting relationships," he told her with a grin.

She understood that. Tess always had Cag put a cover over the albino python's tank before she cleaned his room. That had been the first of many strikes against her. She had a mortal terror of snakes from childhood, having been almost bitten by rattlesnakes several times before her father realized she couldn't see three feet in front of her. Glasses had followed, but the minute she was old enough to protest, she insisted on getting contact lenses.

"Love me, love my enormous terrifying snake, hmm?" she commented. "Well, at least he found someone who was willing to, at first."

"She didn't like Herman, either," he replied. "She told

Cag that she wasn't sharing him with a snake. When they got married, he was going to give him to a man who breeds albinos.''

''I see.'' It was telling that Cag would give in to a woman. She'd never seen him give in to anyone in the months she and her father had been at the ranch.

''He gives with both hands,'' he said quietly. ''If he didn't come across as a holy terror, he wouldn't have a shirt left. Nobody sees him as the soft touch he really is.''

''He's the last man in the world I'd think of as a giver.''

''You don't know him,'' Leo said.

''No, of course I don't,'' she returned.

''He's another generation from you,'' he mused, watching her color. ''Now, I'm young and handsome and rich and I know how to show a girl a good time without making an issue of it.''

Her eyebrows rose. ''You're modest, too!''

He grinned. ''You bet I am! It's my middle name.'' He leaned against the counter, looking rakish. He was really the handsomest of the brothers, tall and big with blond-streaked brown hair and dark eyes. He didn't date a lot, but there were always hopeful women hanging around. Tess thought privately that he was probably something of a rake. But she was out of the running. Or so she thought. It came as a shock when he added, ''So how about dinner and a movie Friday night?''

She didn't accept at once. She looked worried. ''Look, I'm the hired help,'' she said. ''I wouldn't feel comfortable.''

Both eyebrows went up in an arch. ''Are we despots?''

She smiled. ''Of course not. I just don't think it's a good idea, that's all.''

''You have your own quarters over the garage,'' he said

pointedly. "You aren't living under the roof with us in sin, and nobody's going to talk if you go out with one of us."

"I know."

"But you still don't want to go."

She smiled worriedly. "You're very nice."

He looked perplexed. "I am?"

"Yes."

He took a slow breath and smiled wistfully. "Well, I'm glad you think so." Accepting defeat, he moved away from the counter. "Dinner was excellent, by the way. You're a terrific cook."

"Thanks. I enjoy it."

"How about making another pot of coffee? I've got to help Cag with the books and I hate it. I'll need a jolt of caffeine to get me through the night."

"He's going to come home and work through Christmas Eve, too?" she exclaimed.

"Cag always works, as you'll find out. In a way it substitutes for all that he hasn't got. He doesn't think of it as work, though. He likes business."

"To each his own," she murmured.

"Amen." He tweaked her curly red-gold hair. "Don't spend the night in the kitchen. You can watch one of the new movies on pay-per-view in the living room, if you like. Rey's going to visit one of his friends who's in town for the holidays, and Cag and I won't hear the television from the study."

"Have the others gone?"

"Leo wouldn't say where he was going, but Corrigan's taken Dorie home for their own celebration." He smiled. "I never thought I'd see my big brother happily married. It's nice."

"So are they."

He hesitated at the door and glanced back at her. "Is Cag nice?"

She shifted. "I don't know."

A light flickered in his eyes and went out. She wasn't all that young, but she was innocent. She didn't realize that she'd classed him with the married brother. No woman who found him attractive was going to refer to him as "nice." It killed his hopes, but it started him thinking in other directions. Cag was openly hostile to Tess, and she backed away whenever she saw him coming. It was unusual for Cag to be that antagonistic, especially to someone like Tess, who was sensitive and sweet.

Cag was locked tight inside himself. The defection of his fiancée had left Cag wounded and twice shy of women, even of little Tess who didn't have a sophisticated repertoire to try on him. His bad humor had started just about the time she'd come into the house to work, and it hadn't stopped. He had moods during the months that reminded him of when he went off to war and when his engagement had been broken. But they didn't usually last more than a day. This one was lasting all too long. For Tess's sake, he hoped it didn't go on indefinitely.

Christmas Day was quiet. Not surprisingly, Cag worked through it, too, and the rest of the week that followed. Simon and Tira married, a delightful event.

Callaghan's birthday was the one they didn't celebrate. The brothers said that he hated parties, cakes and surprises, in that order. But Tess couldn't believe that the big man wanted people to forget such a special occasion. So Saturday morning after breakfast, she baked a birthday cake, a chocolate one because she'd noticed him having a slice of one that Dorie had baked a few weeks ago. None of the Hart boys were keen on sweets, which they rarely ate.

She'd heard from the former cook, Mrs. Culbertson, that it was probably because their own mother never baked. She'd left the boys with their father. It gave Tess something in common with them, because her mother had deserted her, too.

She iced the cake and put Happy Birthday on the top. She put on just one candle instead of thirty-eight. She left it on the table and went out to the mailbox, with the cat trailing behind her, to put a few letters that the brothers' male secretary had left on the hall table in the morning mail.

She hadn't thought any of the brothers would be in until the evening meal, because a sudden arctic wave had come south to promote an unseasonal freeze. All the hands were out checking on pregnant cows and examining water heaters in the cattle troughs to make sure they were working. Rey had said they probably wouldn't stop for lunch.

But when she got back to the kitchen, her new leather coat tight around her body, she found Callaghan in the kitchen and the remains of her cake, her beautiful cake, on the floor below a huge chocolate spot on the kitchen wall.

He turned, outraged beyond all proportion, looking broader than usual in his shepherd's coat. His black eyes glittered at her from under his wide-brimmed Stetson. "I don't need reminding that I'm thirty-eight," he said in a soft, dangerous tone. "And I don't want a cake, or a party, or presents. I want nothing from you! Do you understand?"

The very softness of his voice was frightening. She noticed that, of all the brothers, he was the one who never yelled or shouted. But his eyes were even more intimidating than his cold tone.

"Sorry," she said in a choked whisper.

"You can't find a damned jar of apple butter for the biscuits, but you've got time to waste on things like...that!" he snapped, jerking his head toward the ruin of her cake lying shattered on the pale yellow linoleum.

She bit her lower lip and stood just looking at him, her blue eyes huge in her white face, where freckles stood out like flecks of butter in churned milk.

"What the hell possessed you? Didn't they tell you I hate birthdays, damn it?"

His voice cut her like a whip. His eyes alone were enough to make her knees wobble, burning into her like black flames. She swallowed. Her mouth was so dry she wondered why her tongue didn't stick to the roof of it. "Sorry," she said again.

Her lack of response made him wild. He glared at her as if he hated her.

He took a step toward her, a violent, quick movement, and she backed up at once, getting behind the chopping block near the wall.

Her whole posture was one of fear. He stopped in his tracks and stared at her, scowling.

Her hands gripped the edge of the block and she looked young and hunted. She bit her lower lip, waiting for the rest of the explosion that she knew was coming. She'd only wanted to do something nice for him. Maybe she'd also wanted to make friends. It had been a horrible mistake. It was blatantly obvious that he didn't want her for a friend.

"Hey, Cag, could you—" Rey stopped dead in his tracks as he opened the kitchen door and took in the scene with a glance. Tess, white-faced, all but shivering and not from the cold. Cag, with his big hands curled into fists at his side, his black eyes blazing. The cake, shattered against a wall.

Cag seemed to jerk as if his brother's appearance had jolted him out of the frozen rage that had held him captive.

"Here, now," Rey said, talking quietly, because he knew his brother in these flash-fire tempers. "Don't do this. Cag, look at her. Come on, look at her, Cag."

He seemed to come to his senses when he caught the bright glimmer of unshed tears in those blue, blue eyes. She was shaking, visibly frightened.

He let out a breath and his fists unclenched. Tess was swallowing, as if to keep her fear hidden, and her hands were pushed deep into the pockets of her coat. She was shaking and she could barely get a breath of air.

"We have to get those culls ready to ship." Rey was still speaking softly. "Cag, are you coming? We can't find the manifest and the trucks are here for the cattle."

"The manifest." Cag took a long breath. "It's in the second drawer of the desk, in the folder. I forgot to put it back in the file. Go ahead. I'll be right with you."

Rey didn't budge. Couldn't Cag see that the girl was terrified of him?

He eased around his brother and went to the chopping block, getting between the two of them.

"You need to get out of that coat. It's hot in here!" Rey said, forcing a laugh that he didn't feel. "Come on, pilgrim, shed the coat."

He untied it and she let him remove it, her eyes going to his chest and resting there, as if she'd found refuge.

Cag hesitated, but only for an instant. He said something filthy in elegant Spanish, turned on his heel and went out, slamming the door behind him.

Tess slumped, a convulsive shudder leaving her sick. She wiped unobtrusively at her eyes.

"Thanks for saving me," she said huskily.

"He's funny about birthdays," he said quietly. "I don't

guess we made it clear enough for you, but at least he didn't throw the cake *at* you,'' he added with a grin. "Old Charlie Greer used to bake for us before we found Mrs. Culbertson, whom you replaced. Charlie made a cake for Cag's birthday and ended up wearing it.''

"Why?'' she asked curiously.

"Nobody knows. Except maybe Simon,'' he amended. "They were older than the rest of us. I guess it goes back a long way. We don't talk about it, but I'm sure you've heard some of the gossip about our mother.''

She nodded jerkily.

"Simon and Corrigan got past the bad memories and made good marriages. Cag…'' He shook his head. "He was like this even when he got engaged. And we all thought that it was more a physical infatuation than a need to marry. She was, if you'll pardon the expression, the world's best tease. A totally warped woman. Thank God she had enough rope to hang herself before he ended up with her around his neck like an albatross.''

She was still getting her breath back. She took the coat that Rey was holding. "I'll put it up. Thanks.''

"He'll apologize eventually,'' he said slowly.

"It won't help.'' She smoothed over the surface of the leather coat. She looked up, anger beginning to replace fear and hurt. "I'm leaving. I'm sorry, but I can't stay here and worry about any other little quirks like that. He's scary.''

He looked shocked. "He wouldn't have hit you,'' he said softly, grimacing when he saw quick tears film her eyes. "Tess, he'd never! He has rages. None of us really understand them, because he won't talk about what's happened to him, ever. But he's not a maniac.''

"No, of course not. He just doesn't like me.''

Rey wished he could dispute that. It was true, Cag was

overtly antagonistic toward her, for reasons that none of the brothers understood.

"I hope you can find someone to replace me," she said with shaky pride. "Because I'm going as soon as I get packed."

"Tess, not like this. Give it a few days."

"No." She went to hang up her coat. She'd had enough of Callaghan Hart. She wouldn't ever get over what he'd said, the way he'd looked at her. He'd frightened her badly and she wasn't going to work for with a man who could go berserk over a cake.

Chapter Two

Rey went out to the corral where the culls—the nonproducing second-year heifers and cows—were being held, along with the young steers fattened and ready for market. Both groups were ready to be loaded into trucks and taken away to their various buyers. A few more steers than usual had been sold because drought had limited the size of the summer corn and hay crop. Buying feed for the winter was not cost-productive. Not even an operation the size of the Harts's could afford deadweight in these hard economic times.

Cag was staring at the milling cattle absently, his heavy brows drawn down in thought, his whole posture stiff and unapproachable.

Rey came up beside him, half a head shorter, lither and more rawboned than the bigger man.

"Well, she's packing," he said bluntly.

Cag's eyes glanced off his brother's and went back to the corral. His jaw clenched. "I hate birthdays! I know she was told."

"Sure she was, but she didn't realize that breaking the rule was going to be life-threatening."

"Hell!" Cag exploded, turning with black-eyed fury. "I never raised a hand to her! I wouldn't, no matter how mad I got."

"Would you need to?" his brother asked solemnly. "Damn it, Cag, she was shaking like a leaf. She's just a kid, and it's been a rough few months for her. She hasn't even got over losing her dad yet."

"Lay it on," Cag said under his breath, moving restlessly.

"Where's she going to go?" he persisted. "She hasn't seen her mother since she was sixteen years old. She has no family, no friends. Even cooking jobs aren't that thick on the ground this time of year, not in Jacobsville."

Cag took off his hat and wiped his forehead on his sleeve before he replaced it. He'd been helping run the steers down the chute into the loading corral and he was sweating, despite the cold. He didn't say a word.

Leo came up with a rope in his hand, watching his brothers curiously.

"What's going on?" he asked.

"Oh, nothing," Rey muttered, thoroughly disgusted. "Tess made him a birthday cake and he destroyed it. She's packing."

Leo let out a rough sigh and turned his eyes toward the house. "I can't say I blame her. I got her into trouble at the Christmas party by spiking the holiday punch, and now this. I guess she thinks we're all lunatics and she's better off without us."

"No doubt." Rey shrugged. "Well, let's get the cattle loaded."

"You aren't going to try to stop her?" Leo asked.

"What would be the point?" Rey asked solemnly. His

face hardened. "If you'd seen her, you wouldn't want to stop her." He glared at Cag. "Nice work, pal. I hope she can pack with her hands shaking that badly!"

Rey stormed off toward the truck. Leo gave his older brother a speaking glance and followed.

Cag, feeling two inches high and sick with himself, turned reluctantly and went back toward the house.

Tess had her suitcases neatly loaded. She closed the big one, making one last sweep around the bedroom that had been hers for the past few weeks. It was a wrench to leave, but she couldn't handle scenes like that. She'd settle for harder work in more peaceful surroundings. At least, Cag wouldn't be around to make her life hell.

She picked up her father's world champion gold belt buckle and smoothed her fingers over it. She took it everywhere with her, like a lucky talisman to ward off evil. It hadn't worked today, but it usually did. She put it gently into the small suitcase and carefully closed the lid, snapping the latches shut.

A sound behind her caught her attention and she turned around, going white in the face when she saw who had opened the door.

She moved around the bed and behind the wing chair that stood near the window, her eyes wide and unblinking.

He was bareheaded. He didn't speak. His black eyes slid over her pale features and he took a long, deep breath.

"You don't have anywhere to go," he began.

It wasn't the best of opening gambits. Her chin went up. "I'll sleep at a Salvation Army shelter," she said coldly. "Dad and I spent a lot of nights there when we were on the road and he didn't win any events."

He scowled. "What?"

She hated having admitted that, to him of all people.

Her face closed up. "Will you let one of the hands drive me to town? I can catch a bus up to Victoria."

He shoved his hands into the pockets of his close-fitting jeans, straining the fabric against his powerful thighs. He stared at her broodingly.

"Never mind," she said heavily. "I'll walk or hitch a ride."

She picked up her old coat, the threadbare tweed one she'd had for years, and slipped it on.

"Where's your new coat?" he asked shortly.

"In the hall closet. Don't worry, I'm not taking anything that doesn't belong to me."

She said it so matter-of-factly that he was wounded right through. "We gave it to you," he said.

Her eyes met his squarely. "I don't want it, or a job, or anything else you gave me out of pity."

He was shocked. He'd never realized she thought of it like that. "You needed a job and we needed a cook," he said flatly. "It wasn't pity."

She shrugged and seemed to slouch. "All right, have it any way you like. It doesn't matter."

She slipped her shoulder bag over her arm and picked up her worn suitcases, one big one and an overnight bag, part of a matched set of vinyl luggage that she and her father had won in a raffle.

But when she reached the door, Cag didn't move out of the way. She couldn't get around him, either. She stopped an arm's length away and stared at him.

He was trying to think of a way to keep her without sacrificing his pride. Rey was right; she was just a kid and he'd been unreasonable. He shocked himself lately. He was a sucker for helpless things, for little things, but he'd been brutal to this child and he didn't know why.

"Can I get by, please?" she asked through stiff lips.

He scowled. A muscle jumped beside his mouth. He moved closer, smiling coldly with self-contempt when she backed up. He pushed the door shut.

She backed up again, her eyes widening at the unexpected action, but he didn't come any closer.

"When I was six," he said with cold black eyes, "I wanted a birthday cake like the other kids had. A cake and a party. Simon had gone to town with Dad and Corrigan. It was before Rey was born. Leo was asleep and my mother and I were in the kitchen alone. She made some pert remark about spoiled brats thinking they deserved treats when they were nothing but nuisances. She had a cake on the counter, one that a neighbor had sent home with Dad. She smashed the cake into my face," he recalled, his eyes darker than ever, "and started hitting me. I don't think she would have stopped, except that Leo woke up and started squalling. She sent me to my room and locked me in. I don't know what she told my father, but I got a hell of a spanking from him." He searched her shocked eyes. "I never asked for another cake."

She put the suitcases down slowly and shocked him by walking right up to him and touching him lightly on the chest with a shy, nervous little hand. It didn't occur to him that he'd never confessed that particular incident to anyone, not even his brothers. She seemed to know it, just the same.

"My father couldn't cook. He opened cans," she said quietly. "I learned to cook when I was eleven, in self-defense. My mother wouldn't have baked me a cake, either, even if she'd stayed with us. She didn't want me, but Dad did, and he put her into a position where she had to marry him. She never forgave either of us for it. She left before I started school."

"Where is she now?"

She didn't meet his eyes. "I don't know. I don't care."

His chest rose and fell roughly. She made him uncomfortable. He moved back, so that her disturbing hand fell away from his chest.

She didn't question why he didn't like her to touch him. It had been an impulse and now she knew not to do it again. She lifted her face and searched his dark eyes. "I know you don't like me," she said. "It's better if I get a job somewhere else. I'm almost twenty-two. I can take care of myself."

His eyes averted to the window. "Wait until spring," he said stiffly. "You'll have an easier time finding work then."

She hesitated. She didn't really want to go, but she couldn't stay here with such unbridled resentment as he felt for her.

He glanced down at her with something odd glittering in his black eyes. "My brothers will drown me if I let you walk out that door," he said curtly. "Neither of them is speaking to me."

They both knew that he didn't care in the least what his brothers thought of him. It was a peace initiative.

She moved restlessly. "Dorie's had the baby. She can make biscuits again."

"She won't," he said curtly. "She's too busy worshiping the baby."

Her gaze dropped to the floor. "It's a sweet baby."

A wave of heat ran through his body. He turned and started back toward the door. "Do what you please," he said.

She still hesitated.

He opened the door and turned before he went through it, looking dark as thunder and almost as intimidating.

"Too afraid of me to stay?" he drawled, hitting her right in her pride with deadly accuracy.

She drew herself up with smoldering fury. "I am *not* afraid of you!"

His eyebrows arched. "Sure you are. That's why you're running away like a scared kid."

"I wasn't running! I'm not a scared kid, either!"

That was more like it. He could manage if she fought back. He couldn't live with the image of her white and shaking and backing away from him. It had hurt like the very devil.

He pulled his Stetson low over his eyes. "Suit yourself. But if you stay, you'd damned sure better not lose the apple butter again," he said with biting sarcasm.

"Next time, you'll get it right between the eyes," she muttered to herself.

"I heard that."

She glared at him. "And if you ever, ever, throw another cake at me...!"

"I didn't throw it at you," he said pointedly. "I threw it at the wall."

Her face was growing redder by the second. "I spent two hours making the damned thing!"

"Lost apple butter, cursed cake, damned women..." He was still muttering as he stomped off down the hall with the faint, musical jingle of spurs following him.

Tess stood unsteadily by the bed for several seconds before she snapped out of her trance and put her suitcases back on the bed to unpack them. She needed her head read for agreeing to stay, but she didn't really have anywhere else to go. And what he'd told her reached that part of her that was unbearably touched by small, wounded things.

She could see a little Cag with his face covered in cake, being brutally hit by an uncaring woman, trying not to cry.

Amazingly it excused every harsh word, every violent action. She wondered how many other childhood scars were hiding behind that hard, expressionless face.

Cag was coldly formal with her after that, as if he regretted having shared one of his deeper secrets with her. But there weren't any more violent outbursts. He kept out of her way and she kept out of his. The winter months passed into a routine sameness. Without the rush and excitement of the holidays, Tess found herself with plenty of time on her hands when she was finished with her chores. The brothers worked all hours, even when they weren't bothered with birthing cattle and roundup, as they were in the warmer months of spring.

But there were fences to mend, outbuildings to repair, upkeep on the machinery that was used to process feed. There were sick animals to treat and corrals to build and vehicles to overhaul. It never seemed to end. And in between all that, there were conferences and conventions and business trips.

It was rare, Tess found, to have all three bachelor brothers at the table at the same time. More often than not, she set places only for Rey and Leo, because Cag spent more and more time away. They assured her that she wasn't to blame, that it was just pressing business, but she wondered just the same. She knew that Cag only tolerated her for the sake of her domestic skills, that he hated the very sight of her. But the other brothers were so kind that it almost made up for Cag. And the ever-present Mrs. Lewis, doing the rough chores, was a fountain of information about the history of the Hart ranch and the surrounding area. Tess, a history buff, learned a lot about the wild old days and stored the information away almost greedily. The lazy,

pleasant days indoors seemed to drag and she was grateful
for any interesting tidbits that Mrs. Lewis sent her way.

Then spring arrived and the ranch became a madhouse.
Tess had to learn to answer the extension phone in the
living room while the two secretaries in the separate office
complex started processing calving information into the
brothers' huge mainframe computer. The sheer volume of
it was shocking to Tess, who'd spent her whole life on
ranches.

The only modern idea, besides the computers, that the
brothers had adapted to their operation was the implanta-
tion of computer chips under the skin of the individual
cattle. This was not only to identify them with a handheld
computer, but also to tag them in case of rustling—a sad
practice that had continued unabashed into the computer
age.

On the Hart ranch, there were no hormone implants, no
artificial insemination, no unnecessary antibiotics or pesticides. The brothers didn't even use pesticides on their
crops, having found ways to encourage the development
of superior strains of forage and the survival of good in-
sects that kept away the bad ones. It was all very ecolog-
ical and fascinating, and it was even profitable. One of the
local ranchers, J. D. Langley, worked hand in glove with
them on these renegade methods. They shared ideas and
investment strategies and went together as a solid front to
cattlemen's meetings. Tess found J. D. ''Donavan'' Langley intimidating, but his wife and nephew had softened
him, or so people said. She shuddered to think how he'd
been before he mellowed.

The volume of business the brothers did was over-
whelming. The telephone rang constantly. So did the fax
machine. Tess was press-ganged into learning how to op-
erate that, and the computer, so that she could help send

and receive urgent e-mail messages to various beef producers and feedlots and buyers.

"But I'm not trained!" she wailed to Leo and Rey.

They only grinned. "There, there, you're doing a fine job," Leo told her encouragingly.

"But I won't have time to cook proper meals," she continued.

"As long as we have enough biscuits and strawberry preserves and apple butter, that's no problem at all," Rey assured her. "And if things get too hectic, we'll order out."

They did, frequently, in the coming weeks. One night two pizza delivery trucks drove up and unloaded enough pizzas for the entire secretarial and sales staff and the cowboys, not to mention the brothers. They worked long hours and they were demanding bosses, but they never forgot the loyalty and sacrifice of the people who worked for them. They paid good wages, too.

"Why don't you ever spend any money on yourself?" Leo asked Tess one night when, bleary-eyed from the computer, she was ready to go to bed.

"What?"

"You're wearing the same clothes you had last year," he said pointedly. "Don't you want some new jeans, at least, and some new tops?"

"I hadn't thought about it," she confessed. "I've just been putting my wages into the bank and forgetting about them. I suppose I should go shopping."

"Yes, you should." He leaned down toward her. "The very minute we get caught up!"

She groaned. "We'll never get caught up! I heard old Fred saying that he'd had to learn how to use a handheld computer so he could scan the cattle in the low pasture, and he was almost in tears."

"We hired more help," he stated.

"Yes, but there was more work after that! It's never going to end," she wailed. "If those stupid cows don't stop having calves...!"

"Bite your tongue, woman, that's profit you're scoffing at!"

"I know, but—"

"We're all tired," he assured her. "And any day now, it's going to slack off. We're doing compilation figures for five ranches, you know," he added. "It isn't just this one. We have to record each new calf along with its history, we have to revise lists for cattle that have died or been culled, cattle that we traded, new cattle that we've bought. Besides that, we have to have birth weights, weight gain ratios, average daily weight gain and feeding data. All that information has to be kept current or it's no use to us."

"I know. But we'll all get sick of pizzas and I'll forget how to make biscuits!"

"God forbid," he said, taking off his hat and holding it to his heart.

She was too tired to laugh, but she did smile. She worked her way down the long hall toward her room over the garage, feeling as drained as she looked.

She met Cag coming from the general direction of the garage, dressed in a neat gray suit with a subdued burgundy tie and a cream-colored Stetson. He was just back from a trustee meeting in Dallas, and he looked expensive and sophisticated and unapproachable.

She nodded in a cool greeting, and averted her eyes as she passed him.

He stepped in front of her, blocking her path. One big, lean hand tilted her chin up. He looked at her without smiling, his dark eyes glittering with disapproval.

"What have they been doing to you?" he asked curtly.

The comment shocked her, but she didn't read anything into it. Cag would never be concerned about her and she knew it. "We're all putting herd records into the computer, even old Fred," she said wearily. "We're tired."

"Yes, I know. It's a nightmare every year about this time. Are you getting enough sleep?"

She nodded. "I don't know much about computers and it's hard, that's all. I don't mind the work."

His hand hesitated for just an instant before he dropped it. He looked tougher than ever. "You'll be back to your old duties in no time. God forbid that we should drag you kicking and screaming out of the kitchen and into the twentieth century."

That was sarcastic, and she wished she had enough energy to hit him. He was always mocking her, picking at her.

"You haven't complained about the biscuits yet," she reminded him curtly.

His black eyes swept over her disparagingly. "You look about ten," he chided. "All big eyes. And you wear that damned rig or those black jeans and that pink shirt all the time. Don't you have any clothes?"

She couldn't believe her ears. First the brothers had talked about her lack of new clothes, and now he was going to harp on it! "Now, look here, you can't tell me what to wear!"

"If you want to get married, you'll never manage it like that," he scoffed. "No man is going to look twice at a woman who can't be bothered to even brush her hair!"

She actually gasped. She hadn't expected a frontal attack when he'd just walked in the door. "Well, excuse me!" she snapped, well aware that her curly head was untidy. She put a hand to it defensively. "I haven't had time to brush my hair. I've been too busy listing what bull sired what calf!''

He searched over her wan face and he relented, just a little. "Go to bed," he said stiffly. "You look like the walking dead."

"What a nice compliment," she muttered. "Thanks awfully."

She started to walk away, but he caught her arm and pulled her back around. He reached into his pocket, took something out, and handed it to her.

It was a jewelry box, square and velvet-covered. She looked at him and he nodded toward the box, indicating that he wanted her to open it.

She began to, with shaking hands. It was unexpected that he should buy her anything. She lifted the lid to find that there, nestled on a bed of gray satin, was a beautiful faceted sapphire pendant surrounded by tiny diamonds on a thin gold chain. She'd never seen anything so beautiful in her life. It was like a piece of summer sky caught in stone. It sparkled even in the dim shine of the security lights around the house and garage.

"Oh!" she exclaimed, shocked and touched by the unexpected gift. Then she looked up, warily, wondering if she'd been presumtuous and it wasn't a gift at all. She held it out to him. "Oh, I see. You just wanted to show it to me..."

He closed her fingers around the box. His big hands were warm and strong. They felt nice.

"I bought it for you," he said, and looked briefly uncomfortable.

She was totally at sea, and looked it. She glanced down at the pretty thing in her hand and back up at him with a perplexed expression.

"Belated birthday present," he said gruffly, not meeting her eyes.

"But…my birthday was the first of March," she said, her voice terse, "and I never mentioned it."

"Never mentioned it," he agreed, searching her tired face intently. "Never had a cake, a present, even a card."

She averted her eyes.

"Hell!"

The curse, and the look on his face, surprised her.

He couldn't tell her that he felt guilty about her birthday. He hadn't even known that it had gone by until Leo told him two weeks ago. She could have had a cake and little presents, and cards. But she'd kept it to herself because of the way he'd acted about the cake she'd made for him. He knew without a word being spoken that he'd spoiled birthdays for her just as his mother had spoiled them for him. His conscience beat him to death over it. It was why he'd spent so much time away, that guilt, and it was why he'd gone into a jewelers, impulsively, when he never did anything on impulse, and bought the little necklace for her.

"Thanks," she murmured, curling her fingers around the box. But she wouldn't look at him.

There was something else, he thought, watching her posture stiffen. Something…

"What is it?" he asked abruptly.

She took a slow breath. "When do you want me to leave?" she asked bravely.

He scowled. "When do I what?"

"You said, that day I baked the cake, that I could go in the spring," she reminded him, because she'd never been able to forget. "It's spring."

He scowled more and stuck one hand into his pocket, thinking fast. "How could we do without you during roundup?" he asked reasonably. "Stay until summer."

She felt the box against her palms, warm from his body where it had lain in his pocket. It was sort of like a link between them, even if he hadn't meant it that way. She'd never had a present from a man before, except the coat the brothers had given her. But that hadn't been personal like this. She wasn't sure how it was intended, as a sort of conscience-reliever or a genuinely warm gesture.

"We'll talk about it another time," he said after a minute. "I'm tired and I've still got things to do."

He turned and walked past her without looking back. She found herself watching him helplessly with the jewelery box held like a priceless treasure in her two hands.

As if he felt her eyes he stopped suddenly, at the back door, and only his head pivoted. His black eyes met hers in the distance between them, and it was suddenly as if lightning had struck. She felt her knees quivering under her, her heart racing. He was only looking, but she couldn't get her breath at all.

He didn't glance away, and neither did she. In that instant, she lost her heart. She felt him fight to break the contact of their eyes, and win. He moved away quickly, into the house, and she ground her teeth together at this unexpected complication.

Of all the men in the world to become infatuated with, Cag Hart was the very last she should have picked. But knowing it didn't stop the way she felt. With a weary sigh, she turned and went back toward her room. She knew she wouldn't sleep, no matter how tired she was. She linked the necklace around her neck and admired it in the mirror, worrying briefly about the expense, because she'd seen on the clasp that it was 14K gold—not a trifle at all. But it would have been equally precious to her if it had been gold-tone metal, and she was sure Cag knew it. She went to sleep, wearing it.

Chapter Three

Everything would have been absolutely fine, except that she forgot to take the necklace off the next morning and the brothers gave her a hard time over breakfast. That, in turn, embarrassed Cag, who stomped out without his second cup of coffee, glaring at Tess as if she'd been responsible for the whole thing.

They apologized when they realized that they'd just made a bad situation worse. But as the day wore on, she wondered if she shouldn't have left the necklace in its box in her chest of drawers. It had seemed to irritate Cag that she wanted to wear it. The beautiful thing was so special that she could hardly get past mirrors. She loved just looking at it.

Her mind was so preoccupied with her present that she didn't pay close attention to the big aquarium in Cag's room when she went to make the bed. And that was a mistake. She was bending over to pull up the multicolored Navajo patterned comforter on the big four-postered bed when she heard a faint noise. The next thing she knew, she was wearing Herman the python around her neck.

The weight of the huge reptile buckled her knees. Herman weighed more than she did by about ten pounds. She screamed and wrestled, and the harder she struggled the harder an equally frightened Herman held on, certain that he was going to hit the floor bouncing if he relaxed his clinch one bit!

Leo came running, but he stopped at the doorway. No snake-lover, he hadn't the faintest idea how to extricate their housekeeper from the scaly embrace she was being subjected to.

"Get Cag!" she squeaked, pulling at Herman's coils. "Hurry, before he eats me!"

"He won't eat you," Leo promised from a pale face. "He only eats freeze-dried dead things with fur, honest! Cag's at the corral. We were just going to ride out to the line camp. Back in a jiffy!"

Stomping feet ran down the hall. Torturous minutes later, heavier stomping feet ran back again.

Tess was kneeling with the huge reptile wrapped around her, his head arched over hers so that she looked as if she might be wearing a snaky headdress.

"Herman, for Pete's sake!" Cag raged. "How did you get out *this* time?"

"Could you possibly question him later, *after* you've got him off me?" she urged. "He weighs a ton!"

"There, there," he said gently, because he knew how frightened she was of Herman. He approached them slowly, careful not to spook his pet. He smoothed his big hand under the snake's chin and stroked him gently, soothing him as he spoke softly, all the time gently unwinding him from Tess's stooped shoulders.

When he had him completely free, he walked back to

the aquarium and scowled as he peered at the lid, which was ajar.

"Maybe he's got a crowbar in there," he murmured, shifting Herman's formidable weight until he could release the other catches enough to lift the lid from the tank. "I don't know why he keeps climbing out."

"How would you like to live in a room three times your size with no playmates?" she muttered, rubbing her aching shoulders. "He's sprained both my shoulders and probably cracked part of my spine. He fell on me!"

He put Herman in the tank and locked the lid before he turned. "Fell?" He scowled. "From where?"

"There!"

She gestured toward one of the wide, tall sculptured posts that graced his king-size bed.

He whistled. "He hasn't gone climbing in a while." He moved a little closer to her and his black eyes narrowed. "You okay?"

"I told you," she mumbled, "I've got fractured bones everywhere!"

He smiled gently. "Sore muscles, more likely." His eyes were quizzical, soft. "You weren't really scared, were you?"

She hesitated. Then she smiled back, just faintly. "Well, no, not really. I've sort of got used to him." She shrugged. "He feels nice. Like a thick silk scarf."

Cag didn't say a word. He just stood there, looking at her, with a sort of funny smile.

"I thought they were slimy."

The smile widened. "Most people do, until they touch one. Snakes are clean. They aren't generally violent unless they're provoked, or unless they're shedding or they've just eaten. Half the work is knowing when not to pick them up." He took off his hat and ran a hand through his thick hair. "I've had Herman for twelve years," he added. "He's like family, although most people don't understand that you can have affection for a snake."

She studied his hard face, remembering that his former fiancée had insisted that he get rid of Herman. Even if he loved a woman, it would be hard for him to give up a much-loved pet.

"I used to have an iguana," she said, "when I was about twelve. One of the guys at the rodeo had it with him, and he was going off to college. He asked would I like him." She smiled reminiscently. "He was green and huge, like some prehistoric creature, like a real live dragon. He liked shredded squash and bananas and he'd let you hold him. When you petted him on the head he'd close his eyes and raise his chin. I had him for three years."

"What happened?"

"He just died," she said. "I never knew why. The vet said that he couldn't see a thing wrong with him, and that I'd done everything right by the book to keep him healthy. We could have had him autopsied, but Dad didn't have the money to pay for it. He was pretty old when I got him. I like to think it was just his time, and not anything I did wrong."

"Sometimes pets do just die." He was looking at Herman, coiled up happily in his tank and looking angelic, in his snaky fashion. "Look at him," he muttered. "Doesn't look like he's ever thought of escaping, does he?"

"I still remember when I opened up the washing machine to do clothes and found him coiled inside. I almost quit on the spot."

"You've come a long way since then," he had to admit. His eyes went to the blue and white sparkle of the necklace and he stared at it.

"I'm sorry," she mumbled, wrapping her hand around

it guiltily. "I never should have worn it around your brothers. But it's so lovely. It's like wearing a piece of the sky around my neck."

"I'm glad you like it," he said gruffly. "Wear it all you like. They'll find something else to harp on in a day or so."

"I didn't think they'd notice."

He cocked an eyebrow. "I haven't bought a present for a woman in almost seven years," he said shortly. "It's noteworthy around here, despite my intentions."

Her face colored. "Oh, I know it was just for my birthday," she said quickly.

"You work hard enough to deserve a treat now and again," he returned impatiently. "You're sure you're okay?"

She nodded. "A little thing like a broken back won't slow me down."

He glowered at her. "He only weighs a hundred and ten pounds."

"Yeah? Well, I only weigh a hundred!"

His eyes went over her suddenly. "You've lost weight."

"You said that before, but I haven't. I've always been thin."

"Eat more."

Her eyebrows arched. "I'll eat what I like, thank you."

He made a rough sound in his throat. "And where are those new clothes we've been trying to get you to buy?"

"I don't want any more clothes. I have plenty of clothes."

"Plenty, the devil," he muttered angrily. "You'll go into town tomorrow and get some new jeans and shirts. Got that?"

She lifted her chin stubbornly. "I will not! Listen here,

I may work for you, but you don't tell me what I can wear!"

He stared at her for a minute with narrowed eyes. "On second thought," he muttered, moving toward her, "why wait until tomorrow? And like hell I can't tell you what to wear!"

"Callaghan!" she shrieked, protesting.

By the time she got his name out of her shocked mouth, he had her over his shoulder in a fireman's lift. He walked right down the hall with her, passing Leo, who was just on his way back in to see what had happened.

"*Oh, my gosh, did Herman bite her?*" he gasped. "Is she killed?"

"No, of course he didn't bite her!" Cag huffed and kept walking.

"Then where are you taking her?"

"To the nearest department store."

"To the...you are? Good man!"

"Turncoat!" Tess called back to him.

"Get her a dress!" Leo added.

"I hate dresses!"

"In that case, get her two dresses!"

"You shut up, Leo!" she groaned.

Rey was standing at the back door when Cag approached it with his burden.

"Going out?" Rey asked pleasantly, and opened the door with a flourish. "Have fun, now."

"Rescue me!" Tess called to him.

"Say, wasn't there a song about that?" Rey asked Leo, who joined him on the porch.

"There sure was. It went like this... 'Rescue me!'" he sang.

The two of them were still singing it, arm in arm, off-key, at the top of their lungs, when Cag drove away in the ranch truck with a furious Tess at his side.

"I don't want new clothes!" she raged.

He glanced toward her red face and grinned. "Too late. We're already halfway to town."

This strangely jubilant mood of his surprised her. Cag, of all the brothers, never seemed to play. Of course, neither did Simon, but he was rarely around. Leo and Rey, she'd been told, had once been just as taciturn as the older Harts. But since Dorie came back into Corrigan's life, they were always up to their necks in something. All Cag did was work. It was completely unlike him to take any personal interest in her welfare.

"Leo could have taken me," she muttered, folding her arms over her chest.

"He's too polite to carry you out the door," he replied. "And Rey's too much a gentleman. Most of the time, anyway."

"These jeans just got broke in good."

"They've got holes in them," he said pointedly.

"It's fashionable."

"Most fashionable jeans have holes in them when you buy them. Those—" he gestured toward the worn knees "—got like that from hard work. I've seen you on your knees scrubbing the kitchen floor. Which reminds me, we bought you one of those little floor cleaners that's specially made for linoleum. They're sending it out with the butane and lumber we ordered at the same time."

"A floor cleaner?" she asked, stunned.

"It will make things a little easier for you."

She was delighted that he was concerned about her chores. She didn't say another word, but she couldn't quite stop smiling.

Minutes later, he pulled up in front of the downtown

department store and led her inside to the women's section. He stopped in front of Mrs. Bellamy, the saleslady who'd practically come with the store.

He tilted his hat respectfully. "Mrs. Bellamy, can you fit her out with jeans and shirts and new boots and a dress or two?" he asked, nodding toward Tess, who was feeling more and more like a mannequin. "We can't have our housekeeper looking like *that!*" He gestured toward her faded shirt and holey jeans.

"My goodness, no, Mr. Hart," Mrs. Bellamy agreed at once. She frowned thoughtfully. "And we just received such a nice shipment of summer things, too! You come right along with me, Miss Tess, and we'll fix you up!" She took Tess's arm and waved her hand at Cag. "Shoo, now, Mr. Hart," she murmured absently, and Tess had to stifle a giggle at his expression. "She'll be ready to pick up in about an hour."

I'm a parcel, Tess thought, and Cag's a fly. She put a hand over her wobbly mouth as she went meekly along with the older woman. Hysterical laughter would not save her now.

Cag watched her go with an amused smile. So she didn't want new clothes, huh? They'd see about that! Mrs. Bellamy wasn't going to let a potential commission walk away from her!

An hour later, Cag went back for Tess and found her trying on a royal blue and white full-skirted dress with spaghetti straps and a shirred bodice. Against her white skin the sapphire-and-diamond necklace was brilliant. With her freckled white shoulders bare and the creamy tops of her breasts showing, she took his breath away.

"Isn't that dress just the thing, Tess?" Mrs. Bellamy was murmuring. "You wait right here. I want to show you one more! Oh, hello, Mr. Hart!'' she called as she passed him. She waved a hand toward Tess. ''What do you think? Isn't it cute? Now where did I see that pretty black lacy thing...''

Tess turned as Cag joined her. His face gave nothing away, but his black eyes glittered over the soft skin left bare by the dress. It certainly made her eyes bluer.

''Is it...too revealing?'' Tess asked nervously, because of the way he was watching her.

He shook his head. ''It suits you. It even matches the necklace.'' His voice sounded deep and husky. He moved closer and one big, lean hand lifted involuntarily to her throat where the small sapphire lay in its bed of diamonds and gold. His hand rested there for an instant before it moved restlessly over the thin strap of the dress. His fingertips absently traced over her soft skin as he studied her, noticing its silky warmth.

Her breath caught in her throat. She felt her heartbeat shaking the dress even as she noticed his black eyes lowering to the flesh left bare by the shirred bodice.

His fingers contracted on her shoulder and her intake of breath was suddenly audible.

He met her eyes relentlessly, looking for hidden signs that she couldn't keep from him.

''This is the sort of dress,'' he said gruffly, ''that makes a man want to pull the bodice down.''

''Mr....Hart!'' she exclaimed.

He scowled faintly as he searched her shocked eyes. ''Don't you know anything about dresses and the effect they have on men?'' he wanted to know.

Her trembling hands went to tug the bodice up even more. ''I do not! But I know that I won't have it if it makes you...makes a man think...such things!''

His hand jerked suddenly, as if her skin had burned it.

"I was teasing!" he lied sharply, moving away. "It's fine. You look fine. And yes," he added firmly, "you'll have it, all right!"

She didn't know what to think. He was acting very strangely, and now he wouldn't look at her at all. Teasing? Then why was he so stiff and uncomfortable looking if he was teasing? And why keep his back to her and Mrs. Bellamy, who'd just rejoined them.

"Here, Tess, try on this one. I'll box that one while you're dressing." She rushed the girl off before she could say anything to Cag.

That was just as well. He was fighting a raging arousal that had shocked him senseless. Tess was beginning to have a very noticeable effect on him, and he was quite sorry that he'd insisted on bringing her here. If she wore that dress around him, it was going to cause some major problems.

He stood breathing deliberately until his rebellious body was back under control. He noticed that Tess didn't show him the black dress she'd tried on. But she shook her head when Mrs. Bellamy asked her about it. She was trying to refuse the blue one, too. He wasn't having that. She looked so beautiful in it. That was one she had to have.

"You're not turning that blue one back in," he said firmly. "You'll need something to wear if you're asked out anywhere." He hated thinking about her in that dress with another man. But she didn't date. It shouldn't worry him. "Did you get some jeans and blouses, and how about those boots?"

After Mrs. Bellamy rattled off an inventory, he produced a credit card and watched her ring up a total. He wouldn't let Tess see it. She looked worried enough already.

He took the two large bags and the dress bag from Mrs. Bellamy with thanks and hustled Tess back out to the double-cabbed truck. He put the purchases on the back seat and loaded Tess into the passenger seat.

She sat without fastening her belt until he got in beside her.

"You spent too much," she said nervously, her big blue eyes echoing her mood. "I won't be able to pay you back for months, even if you take so much a week out of my salary."

"Think of the clothes as a uniform," he said gently. "You can't walk around in what you've been wearing. What will people think of us?"

"Nobody ever comes to see you."

"Visiting cattlemen do. Politicians do. We even have the occasional cookout. People notice these things. And you'll look neater in new stuff."

She shrugged and sighed with defeat. "Okay, then. Thanks."

He didn't crank the truck. He threw a long arm over the back of the seat and looked at her openly. Her barely contained excitement over the clothes began to make sense to him. "You've never had new things," he said suddenly.

She flushed. "On the rodeo circuit, when you lose, you don't make much. Dad and I bought most of our stuff from yard sales, or were given hand-me-downs by other rodeo people." She glanced at him nervously. "I used to compete in barrel racing, and I won third place a few times, but I didn't have a good enough horse to go higher. We had to sell him just before Dad gave up and came here to work."

"Why, Tess," he said softly. "I never knew you could ride at all!"

"I haven't had much chance to."

"I'll take you out with me one morning. Can you ride a quarter horse?"

She smiled. "If he's well trained, sure I can!"

He chuckled. "We'll see, after the biggest part of the roundup's over. We'd never get much done with all the cowboys showing off for you."

She flushed. "Nobody looks at me. I'm too skinny."

"But you're not," he protested. His eyes narrowed. "You're slender, but nobody could mistake you for a boy."

"Thanks."

He reached out unexpectedly and tugged a short reddish-gold curl, bringing her face around so that he could search it. He wasn't smiling. His eyes narrowed as his gaze slid lazily over her eyes, cheekbones and down to her mouth.

"The blue dress suited you," he said. "How did the black one look?"

She shifted restlessly. "It was too low."

"Low what?"

She swallowed. "It was cut almost to the waist. I could never wear something like that in public!"

His gaze fell lower, to the quick rise and fall of her small breasts. "A lot of women couldn't get away with it," he murmured. "But you could. You're small enough that you wouldn't need to wear a bra with it."

"Mr. Hart!" she exclaimed, jerking back.

His eyebrows arched. "I've been Callaghan for months and today I've already been Mr. Hart twice. What did I say?"

Her face was a flaming red. "You...you know what you said!"

He did, all at once, and he chuckled helplessly. He shook his head as he reached for the ignition and switched it on. "And I thought Mrs. Lewis was old-fashioned. You make her look like a hippie!"

She wrapped her arms over her chest, still shaken by

the remark. "You mustn't go around saying things like that. It's indecent!"

He had to force himself not to laugh again. She was serious. He shouldn't tease her, but it was irresistible. She made him feel warm inside, when he'd been empty for years. He should have realized that he was walking slowly toward an abyss, but he didn't notice. He enjoyed having her around, spoiling her a little. He glanced sideways at her. "Put your belt on, honey."

Honey! She fumbled it into the lock at her side, glancing at him uncertainly. He never used endearments and she didn't like them. But that deep, rough voice made her toes curl. She could almost imagine him whispering that word under his breath as he kissed a woman.

She went scarlet. Why had she thought of that? And if the thought wasn't bad enough, her eyes went suddenly to his hard mouth and lingered there in spite of her resolve. She wondered if that mouth could wreak the devastation she thought it could. She'd only been kissed a time or two, and never by anybody who knew how. Callaghan would know how, she was sure of it.

He caught her looking at him and one eyebrow went up. "And what sort of scandalous thoughts are going through that prudish mind now?" he taunted.

She caught her breath. "I don't know what you mean!"

"No?"

"No! And I do not have a prudish mind!"

"You could have fooled me," he said under his breath, and actually grinned.

"Hold your breath until you get any more apple butter with your biscuits," she muttered back. "And wait until you get another biscuit, too!"

"You can't starve me," he said smugly. "Rey and Leo will protect me."

"Oh, right, like they protected me! How could you do that? Carrying me out like a package, and them standing there singing like fools. I don't know why I ever agreed to work for such a loopy family!"

"Loopy? Us?"

"You! You're all crazy."

"What does that make you?" he murmured dryly. "You work for us."

"I need my head read!"

"I'll get somebody on it first thing."

She glanced at him sourly. "I thought you wanted me to quit."

"I already told you, not during roundup!" he reminded her. "Maybe when summer comes, if you're determined."

"I'm not determined. You're determined. You don't like me."

He pursed his lips, staring straight ahead. "I don't, do I?" he said absently. "But you're a fine housekeeper and a terrific cook. If I fired you, the others would stick me in a horse trough and hold me under."

"You destroyed the cake I baked for you," she recalled uneasily. "And you let your snake fall on me."

"That was Herman's own idea," he assured her. His face hardened. "The cake—you know why."

"I know now." She relented. "I'm sorry. I don't know what nice mothers are like, either, because I never had one. But if I had little kids, I'd make their birthdays so special," she said almost to herself, smiling. "I'd bake cakes and give them parties, and make ice cream. And they'd have lots and lots of presents." Her hand went involuntarily to the necklace he'd given her.

He saw that, and something warm kindled in his chest. "You like kids?" he asked without wanting to.

"Very much. Do you?"

"I haven't had much to do with them. I like Mack's toddler, though," he added. The foreman had a little boy two years old who always ran to Cag to be picked up. He always took something over for the child when he went to see Mack and his wife. Tess knew, although he never mentioned it.

She looked out the window. "I don't suppose I'll ever have kids of my own."

He scowled. "Why do you say that?"

She wrapped her arms around her chest. "I don't like...the sort of thing that you have to do to get them."

He stepped on the brakes so hard that the seat belt jerked tight and stared at her intently.

She flushed. "Well, some women are cold!"

"How do you know that you are?" he snapped, hating himself for even asking.

She averted her gaze out the window. "I can't stand to have a man touch me."

"Really?" he drawled. "Then why did you gasp and stand there with your heartbeat shaking you when I slid my hand over your shoulder in the dress shop?"

Her body jerked. "I never!"

"You most certainly did," he retorted, and felt a wave of delight wash over him at the memory of her soft skin under his hands. It had flattered him, touched him, that she was vulnerable with him.

"It was...I mean, I was surprised. That's all!" she added belligerently.

His fingers tapped on the steering wheel as he contemplated her with narrowed eyes. "Something happened to you. What?"

She stared at him, stunned.

"Come on. You know I don't gossip."

She did. She moved restlessly against the seat. "One of

my mother's lovers made a heavy pass at me," she muttered. "I was sixteen and grass green, and he scared me to death."

"And now you're twenty-two," he added. He stared at her even harder. "There aren't any twenty-two-year-old virgins left in America."

"Says who?" she shot at him, and then flushed as she felt herself fall right into the trap.

His lips pursed, and he smiled so faintly that she almost missed it.

"That being the case," he said in a soft, mocking tone, "how do you know that you're frigid?"

She was going to choke to death trying to answer that. She drew in an exasperated breath. "Can't we go home?"

She made the word sound soft, mysterious, enticing. He'd lived in houses all his life. She made him want a home. But it wasn't a thing he was going to admit just yet, even to himself.

"Sure," he said after a minute. "We can go home." He took his foot off the brake, put the truck in gear and sent it flying down the road.

It never occurred to him that taking her shopping had been the last thing on his mind this morning, or that his pleasure in her company was unusual. He was reclusive these days, stoic and unapproachable; except when Tess came close. She was vulnerable in so many ways, like the kitten they'd both adopted. Surely it was just her youth that appealed to him. It was like giving treats to a deprived child and enjoying its reactions.

Except that she trembled under his hands and he'd been years on his own. He liked touching her and she liked letting him. It was something he was going to have to watch. The whole situation was explosive. But he was sure he could handle it. She was a sweet kid. It wouldn't hurt if he spoiled her just a little. Of course it wouldn't.

Chapter Four

The brothers, like Tess and the rest of the staff, were worn to a frazzle by the time roundup was almost over.

Tess hadn't thought Cag meant it when he'd invited her to ride with him while he gathered strays, but early one morning after breakfast, he sent her to change into jeans and boots. He was waiting for her at the stable when she joined him there.

"Listen, I'm a little rusty," Tess began as she stared dubiously toward two saddled horses, one of whom was a sleek black gelding who pranced in place.

"Don't worry. I wouldn't put you on Black Diamond even if you asked. He's mine. This is Whirlwind," he said, nodding toward a pretty little red mare. "She's a registered quarter horse and smart as a whip. She'll take care of you." He summed her up with a glance, smiling at the blue windbreaker that matched her eyes and the Atlanta Braves baseball cap perched atop her red-gold curls.

"You look about ten," he mused, determined to put an invisible Off Limits sign on her mentally.

"And you look about—" she began.

He cut her off in midsentence. "Hop aboard and let's get started."

She vaulted easily into the saddle and gathered the reins loosely in her hands, smiling at the pleasure of being on a horse again. She hadn't ridden since her father's death.

He tilted his tan Stetson over his eyes and turned his mount expertly. "We'll go out this way," he directed, taking the lead toward the grassy path that wound toward the line camp in the distance. "Catch up."

She patted the horse's neck gently and whispered to her. She trotted up next to Cag's mount and kept the pace.

"We do most of this with light aircraft, but there are always a few mavericks who aren't intimidated by flying machines. They get into the brush and hide. So we have to go after those on horseback." He glanced at her jean-clad legs and frowned. "I should have dug you out some chaps," he murmured, and she noticed that he was wearing his own—bat-wing chaps with stains and scratches from this sort of work. "Don't ride into the brush like that," he added firmly. "You'll rip your legs open on the thorns."

"Okay," she said easily.

He set the pace and she followed, feeling oddly happy and at peace. It was nice riding with him like this across the wide, flat plain. She felt as if they were the only two people on earth. There was a delicious silence out here, broken only by the wind and the soft snorting of the horses and occasionally a distant sound of a car or airplane.

They worked through several acres of scrubland, flushing cows and calves and steers from their hiding places and herding them toward the distant holding pens. The men had erected several stockades in which to place the separated cattle, and they'd brought in a tilt-tray, so that the calves could be branded and ear-tagged.

The cows, identified with the handheld computer by the computer chips embedded in their tough hides, were either culled and placed in a second corral to be shipped out, or driven toward another pasture. The calves would be shipped to auction. The steers, already under contract, would go to their buyers. Even so far away from the ranch, there was tremendous organization in the operation.

Tess took off her Braves cap and wiped her sweating forehead on her sleeve.

Hardy, one of the older hands, grinned as he fetched up beside her on his own horse. "Still betting on them Braves, are you? They lost the pennant again last fall...that's two years in a row."

"Oh, yeah? Well, they won it once already," she reminded him with a smug grin. "Who needs two?"

He chuckled, shook his head and rode off.

"Baseball fanatic," Cag murmured dryly as he joined her.

"I'll bet you watched the playoffs last fall, too," she accused.

He didn't reply. "Hungry?" he asked. "We can get coffee and some stew over at the chuck wagon."

"I thought only those big outfits up in the Rockies still packed out a chuck wagon."

"If we didn't, we'd all go hungry here," he told her. "This ranch is a lot bigger than it looks."

"I saw it on the map in your office," she replied. "It sure covers a lot of land."

"You should see our spread in Montana," he mused. "It's the biggest of the lot. And the one that kept us all so busy a few weeks ago, trying to get the records on the computer."

She glanced back to where two of the men were working

handheld computers. "Do all your cowboys know how to use those things?" she asked.

"Most of them. You'd be amazed how many college boys we get here between exams and new classes. We had an aeronautical engineer last summer and a professor of archaeology the year before that."

"Archaeology!"

He grinned. "He spent more time digging than he spent working cattle, but he taught us how to date projectile points and pottery."

"How interesting." She stretched her aching back. "I guess you've been to college."

"I got my degree in business from Harvard."

She glanced at him warily. "And I barely finished high school."

"You've got years left to go to college, if you want to."

"Slim chance of that," she said carelessly. "I can't work and go to school at the same time."

"You can do what our cowboys do—work a quarter and go to school a quarter." He fingered the reins gently. "In fact, we could arrange it so that you could do that, if you like. Jacobsville has a community college. You could commute."

The breath left her in a rush. "You'd let me?" she asked.

"Sure, if you want to."

"Oh, my goodness." She thought about it with growing delight. She could study botany. She loved to grow things. She might even learn how to cultivate roses and do grafting. Her eyes sparkled.

"Well?"

"I could study botany," she said absently. "I could learn to grow roses."

He frowned. "Horticulture?"

"Yes." She glanced at him. "Isn't that what college teaches you?"

"It does, certainly. But if you want horticulture, the vocational school offers a diploma in it."

Her face became radiant at the thought. "Oh, how wonderful!"

"What an expression," he mused, surprised at the pleasure it gave him. "Is that what you want to do, learn to grow plants?"

"Not just plants," she said. *"Roses!"*

"We've got dozens of them out back."

"No, not just old-fashioned roses. Tea roses. I want to do grafts. I want to...to create new hybrids."

He shook his head. "That's over my head."

"It's over mine, too. That's why I want to learn it."

"No ambition to be a professional of some sort?" he persisted. "A teacher, a lawyer, a doctor, a journalist?"

She hesitated, frowning as she studied his hard face. "I like flowers," she said slowly. "Is there something wrong with that? I mean, should I want to study something else?"

He didn't know how to answer that. "Most women do, these days."

"Sure, but most women don't want jobs working in a kitchen and keeping house and growing flowers, do they?" She bit her lip. "I don't know that I'd be smart enough to do horticulture..."

"Of course you would, if you want to do it," he said impatiently. His good humor seemed to evaporate as he stared at her. "Do you want to spend your life working in somebody else's kitchen?"

She shifted. "I guess I will," she said. "I don't want to get married, and I don't really see myself teaching kids or practicing medicine. I enjoy cooking and keeping house.

And I love growing things.'' She glanced at him belligerently. ''What's wrong with that?''

''Nothing. Not a damned thing.''

''Now I've made you mad.''

His hand wrapped around the reins. He didn't look at her as he urged his mount ahead, toward the chuck wagon where several cowboys were holding full plates.

He couldn't tell her that it wasn't her lack of ambition that disturbed him. It was the picture he had of her, surrounded by little redheaded kids digging in the rose garden. It upset him, unsettled him. He couldn't start thinking like that. Tess was just a kid, despite her age, and he'd better keep that in mind. She hadn't even started to live yet. She'd never known intimacy with a man. She was likely to fall headlong in love with the first man who touched her. He thought about that, about being the first, and it rocked him to the soles of his feet. He had to get his mind on something else!

They had a brief lunch with several of the cowboys. Tess let Cag do most of the talking. She ate her stew with a biscuit, drank a cup of coffee and tried not to notice the speculative glances she was getting. She didn't know that it was unusual for Cag to be seen in the company of a woman, even the ranch housekeeper. Certainly he'd never brought anyone female out to a roundup before. It aroused the men's curiosity.

Cag ignored the looks. He knew that having Tess along was innocent, so what did it matter what anyone else thought? It wasn't as if he was planning to drag her off into the brush and make love to her. Even as he thought it, he pictured it. His whole body went hot.

''We'd better get going,'' he said abruptly, rising to his feet.

Tess thanked the cook for her lunch, and followed Cag back to the horses.

They rode off toward the far pastures without a word being spoken. She wondered what she'd done to make Cag mad, but she didn't want to say anything. It might only make matters worse. She wondered if he was mad because she wanted to go back to school.

They left the camp behind and rode in a tense silence. Her eyes kept going to his tall, powerful body. He seemed part of the horse he rode, so comfortable and careless that he might have been born in the saddle. He had powerful broad shoulders and lean hips, with long legs that were sensuously outlined by the tight-fitting jeans he wore under the chaps. She'd seen plenty of rodeo cowboys in her young life, but none of them would have held a candle to Cag. He looked elegant even in old clothes.

He turned his head and caught her staring, then frowned when she blushed.

"Did you ever go rodeoing?" she asked to cover her confusion.

He shook his head. "Never had much use for it," he said honestly. "I didn't need the money, and I always had enough to do here, or on one of the other ranches in the combine."

"Dad couldn't seem to stay in one place for very long," she murmured thoughtfully. "He loved the rodeo circuit, but he didn't win very often."

"It wasn't much of a life for you, was it?" he asked. "It must have been hard to go to school at all."

She smiled. "My education was hit-and-miss, if that's what you mean. But there were these correspondence courses I took so I could get my high school diploma." She flushed deeper and glanced at him. "I know I'm not very educated."

He reined in at a small stream that crossed the wooded path, in the shade of a big oak tree, and let his horse drink, motioning her to follow suit. "It wasn't a criticism," he said. "Maybe I'm too blunt sometimes, but people always know where they stand with me."

"I noticed."

A corner of his mouth quirked. "You aren't shy about expressing your own opinions," he recalled. "It's refreshing."

"Oh, I learned to fight back early," she murmured. "Rodeo's a tough game, and some of the other kids I met were pretty physical when they got mad. I may not be big, but I can kick like a mule."

"I don't doubt it." He drew one long leg up and hooked it over the pommel while he studied her. "But despite all that male company, you don't know much about men."

This was disturbing territory. She averted her gaze to the bubbling stream at their feet. "So you said, when we went to the store." She remembered suddenly the feel of his hard fingers on her soft skin and her heart began to race.

His black eyes narrowed. "Didn't you ever go out on dates?"

Her lithe body shifted in the saddle. "These days, most girls don't care what they do and they're clued up about how to take care of themselves." She glanced at him and away. "It makes it rough for the few of us who don't think it's decent to behave that way. Men seem to expect a girl to give out on the first date and they get mad when she won't."

He traced a cut on his chaps. "So you stopped going out."

She nodded. "It seemed the best way. Besides," she murmured uncomfortably, "I told you. I don't like...that."

"That?"

He was going to worry the subject to death. "That," she emphasized. "You know, being grabbed and forcibly fondled and having a man try to stick his tongue down your throat!"

He chuckled helplessly.

"Oh, you don't understand!"

"In fact, I do," he replied, and the smile on his lips was full of worldly knowledge and indulgent amusement. "You were lucky that your would-be suitors didn't know any more than you did."

She frowned because she didn't understand.

His black eyes searched her face. "Tess, an experienced man doesn't grab. Ever. He doesn't have to. And French kisses need to be worked up to, very slowly."

Her heart was really going now. It shook the cotton blouse she was wearing. She stared at the chaps where Cag's long fingers were resting, and remembered the feel of his lean, strong hands.

"Embarrassed?" he asked softly.

She hesitated. Then she nodded.

His heart jumped wildly as he stared at her, unblinking. "And curious?" he added in a deep, slow drawl.

After a few seconds, she nodded again, but she couldn't make herself meet his eyes.

His hand clenched on the pommel of his saddle as he fought the hunger he felt to teach her those things, to satisfy her curiosity. His gaze fell to her soft mouth and he wanted it. It was crazy, what he was thinking. He couldn't afford a lapse like that. She was just a kid and she worked for him...

She heard the creak of leather as he swung down out of the saddle. After a minute, she felt his lean hands hard on her waist. He lifted her down from the horse abruptly and left the horses to drink their fill.

The sun filtered down to the ground in patterns through the oak leaves there, in the middle of nowhere, in the shelter of the trees where thick grass grew on the shallow banks of the stream and open pasture beyond the spot. The wind whipped around, but Tess couldn't hear it or the gurgle of the stream above the sound of her own heart.

His hands felt rough against her skin. They felt as if he wasn't quite in control, and when she looked up at him, she realized that he wasn't. His face was like steel. The only thing alive in it was those black Spanish eyes, the legacy of a noble Madrid ancestry.

She felt her knees wobble because of the way he was looking at her, his eyes bold on her body, as if he knew exactly what was under her clothing.

The thought of Callaghan Hart's mouth on her lips made her breath catch in her throat. She'd always been a little afraid of him, not because she thought he might hurt her, but because late at night she lay wondering how it would feel if he kissed her. She'd thought about it a lot lately, to her shame. He was mature, experienced, confident, all the things she wasn't. She knew she couldn't handle an affair with him. She was equally sure that he wouldn't have any amorous interest in a novice like her. She'd *been* sure, she amended. Because he was looking at her now in a way he'd never looked at her before.

Her cold hands pressed nervously into the soft cotton of his shirt, feeling the warmth and strength of his chest under it.

"Callaghan," she whispered uncertainly.

His hard lips parted. "Nobody else calls me that," he said tersely, dropping his gaze to her mouth. He liked the way she made his name sound, as if it had a sort of magic.

Her fingers spread. She liked the feel of warm muscle under the shirt, and the soft, spongy feel of thick hair behind the buttons. He was hairy there, she suspected.

He wasn't breathing normally. She could feel his heartbeat against her skin. Her hands pressed gingerly against him, to explore, hesitantly, the hardness of his chest.

He stiffened. His hands on her waist contracted. His breathing changed.

Her hands stilled immediately. She looked up into glittery black eyes. She didn't understand his reactions, never having experienced them before.

"You don't know anything at all, do you?" he asked tersely, and it sounded as if he was talking to himself. He looked down at her short-nailed, capable little hands resting so nervously on top of his shirt. "Why did you stop?"

"You got stiff," she said.

He lifted an eyebrow. "Stiff?"

He looked as if he was trying not to smile, despite the tautness of his face and body.

"You know," she murmured. "Tense. Like you didn't want me to touch you."

He let out a slow breath. His hands moved from her waist to cover her cold fingers and press them closer. They felt warm and cozy, almost comforting. They flattened her hands so that she could feel his body in every cell.

She moved her fingers experimentally where the buttons ran down toward his belt.

"Don't get ambitious," he said, stilling her hands. "I'm not taking off my shirt for you."

"As if I would *ever...!*" she burst out, embarrassed.

He smiled indulgently, studying her flushed face, her wide, bright eyes. "I don't care whether you would, ever, you're not going to. Lift your face."

"Why?" she expelled on a choked breath.

"You know why."

She bit her lip, hard, studying his face with worried eyes. "You don't like me."

"Liking doesn't have anything to do with this." He let go of her hands and gripped her elbows, lifting her easily within reach of his mouth. His gaze fell to it and his chest rose and fell roughly. "You said you were curious," he murmured at her lips. "I'm going to do something about it."

Her hands gripped his shirt, wrinkling it, as his mouth came closer. She could taste the coffee on his warm breath and she felt as if the whole world had stopped spinning, as if the wind had stopped blowing, while she hung there, waiting.

His hard lips just barely touched hers, brushing lightly over the sensitive flesh to savor it. Her eyes closed and she held herself perfectly still, so that he wouldn't stop.

He lifted his head fractionally. She looked as if she couldn't bear to have him draw back. Whatever she felt, it wasn't fear.

He bent again. His top lip nudged under hers, and then down to toy with her lower lip. He felt her gasp. Apparently the kisses she'd had from other men hadn't been arousing. He felt her hands tighten on his shirt with a sense of pure arrogant pleasure.

He brought both lips down slowly over her bottom one, letting his tongue slide softly against the silky, moist inner tissue. She gasped and her mouth opened.

"Yes," he whispered as his own mouth opened to meet it, press into it, parting her lips wide so that he could cover them completely.

She made a tiny sound and her body stiffened, but he ignored the faint involuntary protest. His arms reached down, enclosing, lifting, so that she was completely off the ground in a hungry, warm embrace that seemed to swallow her whole.

The kiss was hard, slow, insistent and delicious. She clasped her hands at the back of Cal's neck and clung to it, her mouth accepting his, loving the hard crush of it. When she felt his tongue slipping past her lips, she didn't protest. She opened her mouth for him, met the slow, velvety thrust with a husky little moan, and closed her eyes even tighter as the intimacy of the kiss made her whole body clench with pleasure.

It seemed a long time before he lifted his head and watched her dazed, misty eyes open.

He searched them in the heady silence of the glade. Nearby a horse whinnied, but he didn't hear it. His heart was beating in time with Tess's, in a feverish rush. He was feeling sensations he'd almost forgotten how to feel. His body was swelling, aching, against hers. He watched her face color and knew that she felt it and understood it.

He eased her back down onto her feet and let her move away a few inches. His eyes never left hers and he didn't let her go completely.

She looked as stunned as he felt. He searched her eyes as his big hand lifted and his fingers traced a blatant path down her breast to the hard tip.

She gasped, but she didn't try to stop him. She couldn't, and he knew it.

His hand returned to her waist.

She leaned her forehead against him while she got her breath back. She wondered if she should be embarrassed. She felt hot all over and oddly swollen. Her mouth was sore, but she wished his hard lips were still covering it. The sensations curling through her body were new and exciting and a little frightening.

"Was it just...a lesson?" she whispered, because she wanted to know.

His hands smoothed gently over her curly head. He stared past it, toward the stream where the horses were still drinking. "No."

"Then, why?"

His fingers slid into her curls. He sighed heavily. "I don't know."

Her eyes closed. She stood against him with the wind blowing all around them and thought that she'd never been so happy, or felt so complete.

He was feeling something comparable, but it disturbed him and made him angry. He hadn't wanted it to come to this. He'd always known, at some level, that it would be devastating to kiss her. This little redhead with her pert manner and fiery temper. She could bring him to his knees. Did she know that?

He lifted his head and looked down at her. She wasn't smiling, flirting, teasing, or pert. She looked as shattered as he felt.

He put her away from him, still holding her a little too tightly by the arms.

"Don't read anything into it," he said shortly.

Her breath was jerky. "I won't."

"It was just proximity," he explained. "And abstinence."

"Sure."

She wasn't humoring him. She really believed him. He was amazed that she didn't know how completely he'd lost control, how violently his body reacted to her. He frowned.

She shifted uneasily and moved back. His hands fell away. Her eyes met his and her thin brows wrinkled. "You won't...you won't tell the brothers?" she asked. She moved a shoulder. "I wouldn't want them to think I was, well, trying to… I mean, that I was flirting or chasing you or…anything.''

"I don't think you're even real," he murmured half-absently as he studied her. "I don't gossip. I told you that. As if I'd start telling tales about you, to my own damned brothers, just because a kiss got a little out of hand!''

She went scarlet. She whirled away from him and stumbled down the bank to catch the mare's reins. She mounted after the second try, irritated that he was already comfortably in the saddle by then, watching her.

"As for the rest of it," he continued, as if there hadn't been any pause between words, "you weren't chasing me. I invited you out here."

She nodded, but she couldn't meet his eyes. What she was feeling was far too explosive, and she was afraid it might show in her eyes.

Her embarrassment was almost tangible. He sighed and rode closer, putting out a hand to tilt up her chin.

"Don't make such heavy weather of a kiss, Tess," he said quietly. "It's no big deal. Okay?''

"Okay." She almost choked on the word. The most earthshaking event of her life, and it was no big deal. Probably to him it hadn't been. The way he kissed, he'd probably worked for years perfecting his technique. But she'd never been kissed like that, and she was shattered. Still, he wasn't going to know it. He didn't even like her, he'd said as much. It had been an impulse, and obviously it was one he already regretted.

"Where do we go next?" she asked with a forced smile.

He scowled. She was upset. He should never have touched her, but it had been irresistible. It had been pure delight to kiss her. Now he had to forget that he ever had.

"The next pasture," he said curtly. "We'll roust out

whatever cattle wildlife we find and then call it a day. You're drooping."

"I guess I am, a little," she confessed. "It's hot."

In more ways than one, he thought, but he didn't dare say it aloud. "Let's go, then."

He rode off, leaving her to follow. Neither of them mentioned what had happened. By the end of the day, they only spoke when they had to. And by the next morning, Cag was glaring at her as if she was the reason for global warming. Everything was back to normal.

Chapter Five

Spring turned to summer. Cag didn't invite Tess to go riding again, but he did have Leo speak to her about starting horticulture classes in the fall.

"I'd really like to," she told Leo. "But will I still be here then?" she added on a nervous laugh. "Cag's worse than ever lately. Any day now, he's going to fire me."

"That isn't likely," Leo assured her, secretly positive that Cag would never let her leave despite his antagonism, because the older man cared too much about her. Oddly Tess was the only person who didn't seem to realize that.

"If I'm still here," she said. "I'd love to go to school."

"We'll take care of it. Cheer up, will you?" he added gently. "You look depressed lately."

"Oh, I'm not," she assured him, lying through her teeth. "I feel just fine, really!"

She didn't tell him that she wasn't sleeping well, because she laid awake nights remembering the way Cag had kissed her. But if she'd hoped for a repeat of that afternoon, it had never come. Cag was all but hostile to her since, complaining about everything from the way she dusted to the way she fastened his socks together in the drawers. Nothing she did pleased him.

Mrs. Lewis remarked dryly that he acted lovesick, and Tess began to agonize about some shadowy woman that he might be seeing on those long evenings when he left the ranch and didn't come home until midnight. He never talked about a woman, but then, he didn't gossip. And even his brothers knew very little about his private life. It worried Tess so badly that even her appetite suffered. How would she survive if Cag married? She didn't like thinking about him with another woman. In fact, she hated it. When she realized why, she felt even worse. How in the world was it that she'd managed to fall in love with a man who couldn't stand to be around her, a man who thought of her only as a cook and housekeeper?

What was she going to do about it? She was terrified that it might show, although she saw no signs of it in her mirror. Cag paid her no more attention than he paid the housecleaning. He seemed to find her presence irritating, though, most especially at mealtimes. She began to find reasons to eat early or late, so that she didn't have to sit at the table with him glaring at her.

Oddly that made things worse. He started picking at her, and not in any teasing way. It got so bad that Leo and Rey took him aside and called him on it. He thought Tess had put them up to it, and blamed her. She withdrew into herself and sat alone in her room at night crocheting an afghan while she watched old black-and-white movies on the little television set her father had given her for Christmas four years ago. She spent less time with the brothers than ever, out of self-defense. But Cag's attitude hurt. She wondered if he was trying to make her quit, even though it was his idea to get her into school in the fall quarter. Perhaps, she thought miserably, he meant her to live in at the school dormitory and quit her job. The thought brought tears to her eyes and made her misery complete.

It was a beautiful summer day when haying got underway on the ranch to provide winter forage for the cattle. It hadn't rained for over a week and a half, and while the danger of drought was ever present, this was a necessary dry spell. The hay would rot in the field if it rained. Besides, it was a comfortable heat, unseasonably cool. Even so, it was hot enough for shorts.

Tess had on a pair of denim cutoffs that she'd made from a torn pair of jeans, and she was wearing socks and sneakers and a gray tank top. She looked young and fresh and full of energy, bouncing across the hayfield with the small red cooler in her hands. She hadn't wanted to go near Cag, but Leo had persuaded her that his older brother would be dying of thirst out there in the blazing sun with nothing to drink. He sent a reluctant Tess out to him with a cooler full of supplies.

Cag, driving the tractor that was scooping the hay into huge round bales, stopped and let the engine idle when he saw her coming toward him. He was alone in the field, having sent two other men into adjacent fields to bale hay in the same fashion. It was blazing hot in the sun, despite his wide-brimmed straw hat. He was bare-chested and still pouring sweat. He'd forgotten to bring anything along to drink, and he hadn't really expected anyone to think about sending him something. He smiled ruefully to himself, certain that Tess wouldn't have thought of it on her own. She was still too nervous of him to come this close willingly, especially considering the way he'd treated her since that unfortunate kiss in the pasture.

It wasn't that he disliked her. It was that he liked her

far too much. He ached every time he looked at her, especially since he'd kissed her. He found himself thinking about it all the time. She was years younger, another generation. Some nice boy would come along and she'd go head over heels. He had to remember that and not let a few minutes of remembered pleasure blind him to reality. Tess was too young for him. Period.

He cut off the tractor and jumped down as she approached him. Her eyes seemed to flicker as they brushed his sweaty chest, thick with black hair that ran down into his close-fitting jeans.

He wiped his hand on a work cloth. "Brought survival gear, did you?" he asked.

"Just a couple of cans of beer and two sandwiches," she said tautly. "Leo asked me to."

"Naturally," he drawled sarcastically. "I'd hardly expect you to volunteer."

She bit her lower lip to keep from arguing with him. She was keenly aware of his dislike. She offered the cooler.

He took it from her, noticing how she avoided touching him as it changed hands.

"Go back along the path," he said, irritated by his own concern for her. "I've seen two big rattlesnakes since I started. They won't like the sun, so they'll be in a cool place. And that—" he indicated her shorts and sneakers "—is stupid gear to wear in a pasture. You should have on thick jeans and boots. Good God, you weren't even looking where your feet were!"

"I was watching the ravens," she said defensively, indicating two of them lighting and flying away in the field.

"They're after field mice." His narrowed black eyes cut into her flushed, averted face. "You're all but shaking. What the hell's wrong with you today?" he demanded.

Her eyes shot back up to his and she stepped back. "Nothing. I should go."

He realized belatedly that the sight of him without his shirt was affecting her. He didn't have to ask why. He already knew. Her hands had been shyly exploring his chest, even through the shirt, the day he'd kissed her, and she'd wanted to unfasten it. But she'd acted as if she couldn't bear to be near him ever since. She avoided him and it made him furious.

"Why don't you run along home?" he asked curtly. "You've done your duty, after all."

"I didn't mind."

"Hell!" He put the cooler down. "You can't be bothered to come within five feet of me unless somebody orders you to." He bit off the words, glaring at her. He was being unreasonable, but he couldn't help himself. "You won't bring me coffee in the office when I'm working unless the door's open and one of my brothers is within shouting distance. What do you expect, you scrawny little redhead, that the sight of you maddens me with such passion that I'm likely to ravish you on the floor? You don't even have a woman's body yet!" he muttered, his eyes on her small, pert breasts under the tank top.

She saw where he was looking and it wounded her. The whiplash of his voice hit her like a brick. She stared at him uncomprehendingly, her eyes wounded. "I never... never said..." she stammered.

"As if you could make me lose my head," he continued coldly, his voice like a sharp blade as his eyes went over her disparagingly.

Her face flamed and the eyes that met his were suddenly clouded not with anger, but with pain. Tears flooded them and she whirled with a sob, running in the direction from which she'd come.

She hated him! *Hated* him! He was the enemy. He'd never wanted her here and now he was telling her that she didn't even attract him. How obvious it was now that he'd only been playing with her when he kissed her. He didn't want her, or need her, or even like her, and she was dying of love for him! She felt sick inside. She couldn't control her tears or the sobs that broke from her lips as she ran blindly into the small sweep of thick hay that he hadn't yet cut.

She heard his voice, yelling something, but she was too upset to hear him. Suddenly her foot hit something that gave and she stopped dead, whirling at a sound like frying bacon that came from the ground beside her.

The ugly flat, venomous head reared as the tail that shot up from the coil rattled its deadly warning. A rattler—five feet long at least—and she'd stepped on it! Its head drew back ominously and she was frozen with fear, too confused to act. If she moved it would strike. If she didn't move it would strike. She could already feel the pain in her leg where the fangs would penetrate....

She was vaguely aware of a drumming sound like running, heavy footsteps. Through her tears she saw the sudden flash of something metallic go past her. The snake and its head abruptly parted company, and then long, powerful arms were around her, under her, lifting her to a sweat-glistening hard chest that was under her cheek.

''God!''

Cag's arms contracted. He was hurting her and she didn't care. Her arms tightened around his neck and she sobbed convulsively. He curled her against him in an ardent fever of need, feeling her soft breasts press hard into his bare, sweaty, hair-roughened chest as his face burrowed into her throat. She thought he trembled, but surely she imagined it. The terror came full force now that the threat was over, and she gave way to her misery.

They clung to each other in the hot sunlight with the sultry breeze wafting around them, oblivious to the man running toward them. Tess felt the warm, hard muscles in his back strain as she touched them, felt Cag's breath in her ear, against her hair. His cheek drew across hers and her nails dug into him. His indrawn breath was audible. His arms contracted again, and this time it wasn't comfort, it was a deep, dragging hunger that found an immediate response in her.

His face moved against hers jerkily, dragging down from her cheek, so that his lower lip slowly, achingly, began to draw itself right across her soft, parted mouth. Her breath drew in sharply at the exquisite feel of it. She wanted his lips on hers, the way they had been that spring day by the stream. She wanted to kiss him until her young body stopped aching.

He hesitated. His hand was resting at the edge of her breast and even as the embrace became hungry, she stopped breathing altogether as she felt his hard lips suddenly part and search for hers, felt the caressing pressure of those lean fingers begin to move up....

On the edge of the abyss, a barely glimpsed movement in the distance brought Cag's dark head up and he saw Leo running toward them. He was almost trembling with the need to take Tess's soft mouth, but he forced himself to breathe normally. All the hot emotion slowly drained out of his face, and he stared at his young brother as if he didn't recognize him for the first few seconds.

"What was it, a rattler?" Leo asked, panting for breath as he came up beside them.

Cag nodded his head toward the snake. It lay in two pieces, one writhing like mad in the hot sun. Between the two pieces was the big hunting knife that Cag always carried when he was working alone in the fields.

"Whew!" Leo whistled, shaking his head. "Pretty accurate, for a man who was running when he threw it. I saw you from the south field," he added.

"I've killed a few snakes in my time," Cag replied, and averted his eyes before Leo could ask if any of them had had two legs. "Here," he murmured to Tess, his voice unconsciously tender. "Are you all right?"

She sniffed and wiped her red eyes and nodded. She was embarrassed, because at the last, it hadn't been comfort that had brought them so close together. It was staggering after the things he said, the harshness of his manner before she'd stepped on the snake.

Cag put her down gingerly and moved back, but his turbulent eyes never left her.

"It didn't strike you?" he asked belatedly, and went on one knee to search over her legs.

"No," she faltered. The feel of those hard fingers on her skin made her weak. "No, I'm fine." She was looking down at him with eyes full of emotion. He was beautiful, she thought dazedly, and when he started to stand up again, her eyes lingered helplessly on that broad, sexy chest with its fine covering of hair. Her hand had touched it just as he put her down, and her fingers still tingled.

"Heavens, Tess!" Leo breathed, taking off his hat to wipe the sweat from his brow. "You don't run across a hayfield like that, without looking where you're going! When we cut hay, we always find half a dozen of the damned things!"

"It's not her fault," Cag said in a surprisingly calm voice. "I upset her."

She didn't look at Cag. She couldn't. She turned to Leo with a wan smile. "Could you walk me back, just to the track that leads up to the house?'' she asked. ''I'm a little shaky.''

''Sure,'' he said gently. ''I'll carry you, if you like.''

''No, I can walk.'' She turned away. With her back to Cag she added carefully, ''Thanks for what you did. I've never seen anybody use a knife like that. It would have had me just a second later.''

Cag didn't say anything. He turned away and retrieved his knife, wiping it on his jeans before he stuck it back into the sheath on his belt. He stalked back toward the tractor. He never looked back.

''What did he do to upset you?'' Leo asked when they were out of earshot.

''The usual things,'' she said with resignation in her voice. ''I can't imagine why he doesn't fire me,'' she added. ''First he said I could go in the spring, but we got too busy, then he said I could go in the summer. But here it is, and I'm still here.''

He didn't mention that he had his own suspicions about that. Cag was in deep, and quite obviously fighting a defensive battle where Tess was concerned. But he'd seen the look on Cag's face when he was holding her, and dislike was not what it looked like to him.

''Did you see him throw the knife?'' she asked, still awed by the skill of it. ''Dad used to have a throwing knife and he could never quite get the hang of hitting the target. Neither could I. It's a lot harder than it looks. He did it running.''

''He's a combat veteran,'' he said. ''He's still in the reserves. Nothing about Cag surprises us anymore.''

She glanced at him with twinkling eyes. ''Did you really hit Turkey Sanders to keep Cag from doing it?''

''Dorie told you!'' He chuckled.

''Yes. She said you don't let Cag get into fights.''

"We don't dare. He doesn't lose his temper much, but when he does, it's best to get out of the line of fire."

"Yes, I know," she said uneasily, still remembering the birthday cake.

He glanced at her. "You've had a hard time."

"With him?" She shrugged. "He's not so bad. Not as bad as he was around Christmas," she added. "I guess I'm getting used to sarcasm and insults. They bounce off these days."

He made a rough sound under his breath. "Maybe he'll calm down eventually."

"It doesn't matter. I like my job. It pays well."

He laughed, sliding a friendly arm around her shoulders as they walked. "At least there are compensations."

Neither of them saw a pair of black eyes across the field glaring after them hotly. Cag didn't like that arm around Tess, not one bit. He was going to have something to say to Leo about it later.

Blissfully unaware, Leo stopped at the trail that led back to the house. "Okay now?" he asked Tess.

"Yes, thanks."

He studied her quietly. "It may get worse before it gets better, especially now," he said with some concern.

"What do you mean?"

"Never you mind," he replied, and his eyes held a secret amusement.

That evening, after the brothers cleaned up and had supper, Cag motioned Leo into the study and closed the door.

"Something wrong?" Leo asked, puzzled by his brother's taciturn silence since the afternoon.

Cag perched himself on the edge of his desk and stared, unblinking, at the younger man.

"Something," he agreed. Now that he was facing the

subject, he didn't want to talk about it. He looked as disturbed as he felt.

"It's Tess, isn't it?" Leo asked quietly.

"She's twenty-two," Cag said evenly, staring hard at his brother. "And green as spring hay. Don't hit on her."

It was the last thing Leo expected the older man to say. "Don't *what?*" he asked, just to make sure he wasn't hearing things.

Cag looked mildly uncomfortable. "You had your arm around her on the way out of the field."

Leo's dark eyes twinkled. "Yes, I did, didn't I?" He pursed his lips and glanced at his brother with pure calculation. "She's a soft little thing, like a kitten."

Cag's face hardened and his eyes became dangerous. "She's off limits. Got that?"

Leo lifted both eyebrows. "Why?"

"Because she's a virgin," Cag said through his teeth. "And she works for us."

"I'm glad you remembered those things this afternoon," Leo returned. "But it's a shame you'd forgotten all about them until you saw me coming toward you. Or are you going to try and convince me that you weren't about to kiss the breath out of her?"

Cag's teeth ground together. "I was comforting her!"

"Is *that* what you call it?" came the wry response. "Son of a gun. I'm glad I have you to tell me these things."

"I wasn't hitting on her!"

Leo held up both hands. "Of course not!"

"If she's too young for you, she's damned sure too young for me."

"Was I arguing?"

Cag unruffled a little. "Anyway, she wants to go to

school and study horticulture in the fall. She may not want to stay on here, once she gets a taste of younger men.''

Why, he really believed that, Leo thought, his attention diverted. Didn't he see the way Tess looked at him, the way she acted around him lately? Or was he trying not to see it?

''She won't have to wait for that to happen,'' Leo murmured. ''We hired a new assistant sales manager last week, remember? Sandy Gaines?''

Cag scowled. ''The skinny blond fellow?''

''Skinny, sure, but he seems to have plenty of charm when it comes to our Tess. He brought her a teddy bear from his last trip to St. Louis, and he keeps asking her out. So far she won't go.''

Cag didn't want to think about Tess with another man, especially the new salesman. ''She could do worse, I guess,'' he said despite his misgivings.

''You might ask her out yourself,'' Leo suggested carelessly.

Cag's dark eyes held a world of cynicism. ''I'm thirty-eight and she works for me.''

Leo only smiled.

Cag turned away to the fireplace and stared down at the gas logs with resignation. ''Does it show?'' he asked after a minute.

That he cared for her, he meant. Leo smiled affectionately. ''Only to someone who knows you pretty well. She doesn't. You won't let her close enough,'' Leo added.

Broad shoulders rose and fell. His eyes lifted to the huge painting of a running herd of horses tearing across a stormy plain. A great-uncle had painted it. Its wildness appealed to the brothers.

''She's grass green,'' Cag said quietly. ''Anybody could turn her head right now. But it wouldn't last. She's too immature for anything…serious." He turned and met his brother's curious eyes. "The thing is," he said curtly, "that I can't keep my head if I touch her."

"So you keep her carefully at a distance to avoid complications."

Cag hesitated. Then he nodded. He stuffed his hands into the pockets of his jeans and paced. "I don't know what else to do. Maybe if we get her into school this fall, it will help. I was thinking we might even get her a job somewhere else."

"I noticed," Leo said dryly. "And then you tell her to wait one more season. She's waited two already."

Cag's black eyes cut into him. "I haven't been serious about a woman since I was sent to the Middle East," he said through his teeth. "I've been pretty bitter. I haven't wanted my heart twisted out of my chest again. Then, she came along." He nodded in the general direction of the kitchen. "With her curly red hair and big blue eyes and that pert little boyish figure." He shook his head as if to clear the image from it. "Damn it, I ache just looking at her!" He whirled. "I've got to get her out of here before I do something about it!"

Leo studied his hand. "Are you sure you don't want to do something about it?" he asked softly. "Because she wants you to. She was shaking when you put her down."

Cag glared at him. "The snake scared her."

"*You* scared her," came the wry response. "Have you forgotten how to tell when a woman's aroused?"

"No, I haven't forgotten," he replied grimly. "And that's why she's got to go. Right now."

"Just hold on. There's no need to go rushing into anything," Leo counseled.

"Oh, for God's sake, it's just a matter of time, don't

you see?'' Cag groaned. "You can't hold back an avalanche!"

"Like that, is it?"

"Worse." Cag lowered his head with a hard sigh. "Never like this. Never."

Leo, who'd never felt what passed for love in the world, stared at his brother with compassion but no real understanding of what he was going through.

"She fits in around here," Leo murmured.

"Sure she does. But I'm not going to marry her!"

Leo's eyebrows lifted. "Why not? Don't you want kids?"

"Corrigan's got one."

"Kids of your own," Leo persisted with a grin. "Little boys with big feet and curly red hair."

Cag lifted a paperweight from the desk and tossed it deliberately in one hand.

Leo held up both hands in a defensive gesture. "Don't throw it. I'm reformed. I won't say another word."

The paperweight was replaced on the desk. "Like I said before, I'm too old for her. After all the other considerations have been taken into account, that one remains. Sixteen years is too much."

"Do you know Ted Regan?"

Cag scowled. "Sure. Why?"

"Do you know how much older he is than Coreen?"

Cag swallowed. "Theirs is a different relationship."

"Calhoun Ballenger and Abby?"

Cag glared at him.

"Evan and Anna Tremayne?"

The glare became a black scowl.

Leo shrugged. "Dig your own grave, then. You should hear Ted groan about the wasted years he spent keeping Coreen at bay. They've got a child of their own now and they're talking about another one in the near future. Silver hair and all, Ted's the happiest fellow I know. Coreen keeps him young."

"I'll bet people talked."

"Of course people talked. But they didn't care."

That grin was irritating. Cag turned away from him. He didn't dare think about kids with curly red hair. He was already in over his head and having enough trouble trying to breathe.

"One day, a young man will come along and sweep her off her feet."

"You've already done that, several times," Leo said pointedly. "Carrying her off to the store to buy new clothes, and just today, out of the path of a rattler."

"She doesn't weigh as much as a good sack of potatoes."

"She needs feeding up. She's all nerves lately. Especially when you're around."

Cag's big hands clenched in his pockets. "I want to move the heifers into the west pasture tomorrow. What do you think?"

"I think it's a week too soon."

The broad shoulders shrugged. "Then we'll wait one more week. How about the pastures on the bottoms?"

"We haven't had rain, but we will. If they flood, we'll have every cowboy on the place out pulling cows out of mud." His eyes narrowed. "You know all that better than I do."

"I'm changing the subject."

Leo threw up his hands. "All right. Don't listen to me. But Sandy Gaines means business. He's flirting with her, hard. He's young and personable and educated, and he wears nice suits and drives a red Corvette."

Cag glared at him. "She can see through clothes and a car, even a nice car."

"She's had digs and sarcasm and insults from you," Leo said and he was serious. "A man who tells her she's pretty and treats her gently might walk up on her blind side. She's warming to him a little. I don't like it. I've heard things about him."

"What sort of things?" Cag asked without wanting to.

"That he's fine until he gets his hands on a bottle of liquor, and then he's every woman's worst nightmare. You and I both know the type. We don't want our Tess getting into a situation she can't handle."

"She wouldn't tolerate that sort of behavior from a man," he said stiffly.

"Of course not, but she barely weighs a hundred pounds sopping wet! Or have you forgotten that she couldn't even get away from Herman, and he only outweighs her by ten pounds? Gaines is almost your size!"

Cag's teeth clenched. "She won't go out with him," he said doggedly. "She's got better sense."

That impression only lasted two more days. Sandy Gaines, a dark-haired, blue-eyed charmer, came by to discuss a new advertising campaign with the brothers and waylaid Tess in the hall. He asked her to a dance at the Jacobsville dance hall that Friday night and she, frustrated and hurt by Cag's sarcasm and coldness, accepted without hesitation.

Chapter Six

Sandy picked her up early for the dance in his low-slung used red Corvette. Cag was nearby and he watched them with cold eyes, so eaten up with jealousy that he could hardly bear it. She was wearing their dress, to top it all, the blue dress he'd helped her pick out when he'd taken her shopping. How could she wear it for that city dude?

"Get her home by midnight," he told Sandy, and he didn't smile.

"Sure thing, Mr. Hart!"

Sandy put Tess into the car quickly and drove off. Tess didn't even look at Cag. She was uncomfortably aware of the dress she had on, and why Cag glared at her. But he didn't want to take her anywhere, after all, so why should he object to her going out on a date? He didn't even like her!

"What's he, your dad?" Sandy drawled, driving far too fast.

"They all look out for me," she said stiffly.

Sandy laughed cynically. "Yeah? Well, he acts like you're his private stock." He glanced at her. "Are you?"

"Not at all," she replied with deliberate carelessness.

"Good." He reached for her hand and pressed it. "We're going to have a nice time. I've looked forward to this all week. You're a pretty little thing."

She smiled. "Thanks."

"Now you just enjoy yourself and don't worry about heavy-handed surrogate parents, okay?"

"Okay."

But it didn't work out that way. The first two dances were fun, and she enjoyed the music. But very quickly, Sandy found his way to the bar. After his second whiskey sour, he became another man. He held her too closely and his hands wandered. When he tried to kiss her, she struggled.

"Oh, no, you don't," he muttered when she tried to sidestep him. He caught her hand and pulled her out of the big structure by a side door. Seconds later, he pushed her roughly up against the wall in the dim light.

Before she could get a hand up, he was kissing her—horrible wet, invasive kisses that made her gag. She tasted the whiskey on his breath and it sickened her even further. His hands grasped her small breasts roughly, hurting, twisting. She cried out and fought him, trying to get away, but his hips levered down over hers with an obscene motion as he laughed, enjoying her struggles as she tried valiantly to kick him.

It was like that other time, when she was sixteen and she'd been at the mercy of another lecherous man. The memories further weakened her, made her sick. She tried to get her knee up, but she only gave him an opening that brought them even more intimately together and frightened her further. She was beating at his chest, raging at him, and his hand was in the neckline of her dress, popping buttons off in his drunken haste, when she felt the pressure against her body suddenly lessen.

There were muffled curses that stopped when Sandy was suddenly pushed up against the wall himself with one arm behind him and a mercilessly efficient hand at his neck, the thumb hard under his ear. Cag looked violent as Tess had rarely seen him. The hold was more than dangerous, it was professional. She didn't have the slightest doubt that he could drop the other man instantly if it became necessary.

"Move, and I'll break your neck," Cag said in a voice like hot steel. His black eyes cut to Tess and took in her disheveled clothing, her torn bodice. He jerked his head toward the ranch pickup that was parked just at the edge of the grass. "It's unlocked. Go and get inside."

She hesitated, sick and wobbly and afraid.

"Go on," Cag said softly.

She turned. She might have pleaded for Sandy, except that she didn't think he deserved having her plead for him. He might have…God only knew what he might have done if Cag hadn't shown up! She resisted the urge to kick him while Cag had him powerless, and she wobbled off toward the truck.

She was aware of dull thuds behind her, but she didn't turn. She went to the truck, climbed in and sat shivering until a cold, taciturn Cag joined her.

Before he got into the cab, he pulled off the denim shirt he was wearing over a black T-shirt and put it over her shoulders the wrong way. He didn't attempt to touch her, probably aware that she was sick enough of being touched at the moment.

"Get into that," he said as he fastened his seat belt, "and fasten your belt."

He reached for the ignition and she noticed that his knuckles were bleeding. As she struggled into the shoulder harness she glanced toward the barn and saw Sandy leaning against the wall, looking very weak.

"I couldn't make him stop," she said in a thin voice. "I didn't expect him to...to get drunk. He seemed so nice. I never go out with big men usually—" Her voice broke. "Damn him! Oh, damn him! I never dreamed he'd be like *that!* He seemed like such a nice man!"

He glanced toward her with a face like black thunder, but he didn't speak. He put the truck in gear and drove her home.

The others were out for the evening. They were alone in the house. She started to go down the hall toward her room, but he turned her into the study and closed the door.

He seated her on the big black antique leather divan that graced the corner near the picture window and went to pour brandy into a snifter.

He came back and sat beside her, easing her cold, trembling hands around the bowl and offering it at her swollen lips. It stung and she hesitated, but he tilted it up again.

She let out a single sob and quickly controlled herself. "Sorry," she said.

"Why did you go out with him?"

"He flattered me," she said with pure self-disgust. "He was sweet to me and he seemed sort of boyish. I thought...I thought he'd be a perfect gentleman, the sort of man I'd never have to fight off. But he was different when we were alone. And then he started drinking."

"You're grass green," he muttered. "You can't size up men even now, can you?"

"I haven't dated much."

"I noticed."

She glanced up at his set features and then down into the brandy.

"Why haven't you?" he persisted.

She tried not to notice how sexy he looked in that black T-shirt that clung to every muscle he had. He was big, lean, all powerful muscle and bristling vitality. It made her weak to look at him, and she averted her eyes.

"My mother came to see us one day, when I was sixteen," she said uneasily. "She wanted to see how much I'd grown up, she said." She shifted. "She brought her latest lover. He was a playboy with lots of money and apparently he saw that it irritated her when he paid me some attention, so he put on the charm and kept it up all day. After supper, she was miffed enough to take my dad off into another room. Dad was crazy about her, even then." She swallowed. "It made her lover furious and vengeful. He closed the door and before I knew what was happening, he locked it and threw me down onto the sofa. He tore my clothes and touched me...." She closed her eyes at the horrible memory. "It was like tonight, only worse. He was a big man and strong. I couldn't get away, no matter how hard I fought, and in the end I just screamed. My father broke in the door to get to him. I'll never forget what he said to that man, and my mother, before he threw them off the place. I never saw her again. Or wanted to."

Cag let out the breath he'd been holding. So many things made sense now. He searched her wan little face with feelings of possession. She'd had so much pain and fear from men. She probably had no idea that tenderness even existed.

"You're tied up in bad memories, aren't you, little one?" he asked quietly. "Maybe they need to be replaced with better ones."

"Do they?" Her voice was sad, resigned. She finished the brandy and Cag put the snifter on the table.

She started to get up, only to find him blocking her way. He eased her back down onto the wide divan and slid down alongside her.

She gasped, wondering if she'd gotten out of the frying pan only to fall into the fire. She frantically put her hands against his broad chest and opened her mouth to protest, but his fingers touched it lightly as he laid beside her and arched over her prone body resting his formidable weight on his forearm.

"There's nothing to be afraid of, Tess," he said quietly. "Whatever disagreements we've had, you know that I'd never hurt you physically. Especially after the ordeal you've just been through."

She knew, but she was still nervous of him. He was even more powerfully built than Sandy, and in this way, in an intimate way, he was also an unknown quantity.

While she was thinking, worrying, he bent and she felt the warm threat of his big body as his mouth drew softly over her eyes, closing the lids. It moved to her temples, her eyebrows. He kissed her closed eyes, his tongue lightly skimming the lashes. She jerked, and his lean hand eased under her nape, soothing her, calming her.

She had little experience, but she wasn't so naive that she couldn't recognize his. Every touch, every caress, was expert. He eased down so slowly that she only realized how close he really was when she moved and felt his warm, hard chest move with her. By then, she was a prisoner of her own sensual curiosity, sedated by the exquisite pleasure his mouth was giving her as it explored her face.

By the time he reached her lips, the feel and smell of him were already familiar. When his hard mouth eased her lips apart and moved into them, she felt the increased pressure of his chest against her breasts, and she stiffened with real fear.

He lifted away immediately, but only a breath. His black eyes searched her blue ones slowly.

"You still don't know me like this," he murmured, as if he were talking to himself as he studied her flushed face, understanding the fear he read in it. "You're afraid, aren't you?"

She swallowed. Her mouth felt dry as she looked at him. "I think I am," she whispered.

He smiled lazily and traced her lips with a lean forefinger. "Will you relax if I promise to go so far and stop?" he whispered.

"So…far?" she asked in a hushed tone, searching his black eyes curiously.

He nodded. He teased her lips apart and touched the inside of her lower lip with the tip of his finger. "We'll make a little love," he whispered as he bent. "And then you'll go to bed. Your own, not mine," he added with dry mischief.

Her fingers clenched and unclenched on the soft fabric of his undershirt, like a kitten kneading a new place to lay. She could hear her own breath sighing out against his mouth as it came closer.

"You don't like me," she breathed.

His thumb rubbed quite roughly over her mouth. "Are you sure? You must know that I want you!" he said, and it came out almost as a growl. "Taunting you was the only way I knew to keep you at arm's length, to protect you. I was a fool! I'm too old for you, but at least I'm not like that damned idiot who took you out tonight!"

Nothing got into her sluggish brain except those first three feverish words. "You want me?" she whispered as if it was some dark secret. She looked up at him with wonder and saw the muted ferocity in his eyes.

His hand was on her waist now and it contracted until it all but bruised. "Yes, Tess. Is it shocking to hear me say it?" His gaze fell to her mouth and lower, to the two little peaks that formed suddenly against the torn bodice of her dress and were revealed even under the thick fabric of his concealing shirt. "You want me, too," he whispered, bending. "I can see it...."

She wanted to ask how he knew, but the taste of his breath against her lips weakened her. She wanted him to kiss her. She wanted nothing more in the world. Her nails curled into his powerful chest and she felt him shiver again just as his mouth slowly, tenderly, eased down on her parted lips.

He drew back almost at once, only to ease down again as his lips toyed with hers, brushing lightly from the upper lip to the lower one, teasing and lifting away in a silence that smoldered. She felt the warm pressure increase from second to second, and the leisure of his movements reassured her. She began to relax. Her body lost its rigor and softened against him. After a few seconds of the lazy, tender pressure, her lips opened eagerly for him. She heard a soft intake of breath as he accepted the unspoken invitation with increasingly intimate movements of his hard mouth.

The spicy fragrance of his cologne surrounded her. She knew that as long as she lived, every time she smelled it, it would invoke these images of Cag lying against her on the leather divan in the muted light of the study. She would hear the soft creak of the leather as his body moved closer to her own; she would hear the faint ticking of the old-fashioned grandfather clock near the desk. Most of all, she would feel the hard warmth of Cag's mouth and the slow caress of his lean hands up and down her rib cage, making her body ache with new pleasures.

His head lifted and he looked at her again, this time reading with pinpoint accuracy the sultry look of her eyes, the faint pulse in her throat, the hard tips of her breasts rising against the slip that her half-open bodice revealed. Somewhere along the way, he'd unbuttoned his shirt that she was wearing and it was lying back away from her torn dress.

He traced the ragged edge of the fabric with returning anger. "Did it have to be this dress?" he groaned.

She winced. "You never seemed to look at me," she defended herself. "He wanted to take me out, and it was the nicest thing I had in my closet."

He sighed heavily. "Yes, I know." He smiled wryly. "I didn't think I could risk taking you out. But look what happened because I didn't."

"He was so drunk," she whispered hoarsely. "He would have forced me..."

"Not while there was a breath in my body," he returned intently.

"How did you know?" she asked suddenly.

He pushed a stray curl away from her cheek. "I don't know," he said, frowning as if it disturbed him. "Something I'd heard about Gaines bothered me. One of the men said that he was fine as long as there wasn't a bottle anywhere nearby, and another one mentioned a threatened lawsuit over a disastrous date. I remembered that you'd gone to the dance at the bar." He shrugged. "Maybe it was a premonition. Thank God I paid attention to it."

"Yes." A thick strand of jet black hair had fallen onto his broad forehead. Hesitantly she reached up and pushed it back, her fingers lingering on its coolness.

He smiled because it was the first time that she'd voluntarily touched him.

She sought his eyes, sought permission. As if he understood the new feelings that were flaring up inside her, he drew her hand down to his chest and opened her fingers, pressing them there, firmly.

Her hand moved experimentally, pressing down and then curling into the thick hair she could feel under the soft fabric of his shirt.

Impatiently he lifted himself and peeled off the T-shirt, tossing it to the floor. He lay back down again beside her, curling his leg into hers as he guided her hand back to his chest.

She hesitated again. This was another step, an even bigger one.

"Even teenagers do this," he mused, smiling gently at her inhibitions. "It's perfectly permissible."

"Is it?" Her fingers touched him as if she expected them to be burned. But then they pressed into the thick pelt of hair and explored, fascinated by the size and breadth of his chest, the warmth and strength of it.

He arched with pure pleasure and laughed delightedly at the sensations she aroused. It had been a long time since a woman had touched him like that.

She smiled shyly, fascinated by his reaction. He seemed so stoic, so reserved, that this lack of inhibition was surprising.

"Men are like cats," he murmured. "We love to be stroked."

"Oh." She studied him as if he were an exhibit in a museum, curious about every single cell of his body.

"Feeling more secure now?" he asked softly. "More adventurous?"

"I'm not sure." She looked up at him, quizzically.

"Nothing heavy," he promised. His black eyes were softer than she'd ever seen them. "It's no news to me that you're a rank beginner."

"What are you…going to do?" she stammered, wide-eyed.

"Kiss you," he breathed, letting his gaze fall to her bare breasts.

"Th…there?" she gasped.

He touched her lightly, smiling at the expression on her taut face. "There," he whispered. He bent and drew his cheek softly over the bruised flesh, careful not to hurt her with the light pressure.

While she was trying to cope with so many new and shocking sensations, his mouth smoothed back over the soft, silky flesh and she felt it open. He tasted her flushed skin in a heated fever of need. Her hands curled up into his thick hair and she held him to her, whimpering softly with pleasure as she found herself drawing his face hungrily to where the flesh was very taut and sensitive.

"Here?" he whispered, hesitating.

"Oh…yes!" she choked.

His mouth opened obediently and he drew the hard nipple into it with a faint, soft suction that brought a sharp cry from her dry lips.

She thought she felt him tremble, and then he was moving onto his back, breathing roughly as he carried her with him. He held her at his side, their legs intimately entangled, while he fought to get his breath back.

His skin was cool against her hot breasts where they were pressed together above the waist. Her cheek was against the hard muscle of his upper arm and she caught again that elusive spicy scent that clung to him.

Her hand eased onto the thick hair at his chest, but he caught it and held it a little roughly at her side.

"No," he whispered.

She didn't understand what she'd done wrong. A minute later, he got to his feet and bent to retrieve his undershirt. While he shrugged into it, she tugged up her bodice and tried to fasten it.

But when she would have gotten to her feet, he pressed her back down.

"Stay put," he said quietly. He turned and left the room.

She'd barely gotten her breathing calm when he was back, sitting down beside her with a cold can of beer in his hand.

He popped it open and took a sip before he pulled her up beside him and held it to her lips.

"I don't like beer," she murmured dazedly.

"I'm going to taste of it," he replied matter-of-factly. "If you swallow some, you won't find the taste so unpleasant when I kiss you."

Her heart jumped wildly.

He met her surprised expression with a smile. "Did you think we were finished?" he asked softly.

She blushed.

"I was getting too aroused," he murmured dryly. "And so were you. I'm not going to let it go that far."

She searched his hard face with open curiosity. "What does it feel like to you, when you kiss me like that?" she asked quickly, before she lost her nerve.

"How does it feel when I do it?"

"I don't know. Shivery. Hot. I never felt anything like that before."

He took a sip of the beer and looked down at her hungrily. "Neither did I," he said tersely. His eyes seemed to possess her as they ran like caressing hands all over her. "Your breasts are freckled," he said with an intimate smile and chuckled when she blushed. He held her face up to his and kissed her nose. "I'm not going to rush out to the nearest bar and gossip about it," he whispered when he saw the faint apprehension in her wide eyes. "It's a lover's secret; a thing we don't share with other people. Like the scar on my belly."

She frowned slightly. He tugged down the waistband of his jeans and drew her hand against him where a long, thick scar was just visible above his belt.

"It runs down to my groin," he said solemnly. "Fortunately, it missed the more...vital areas. But it was touch and go for a few days and the scar is never going to go away."

Her fingers lingered there. "I'm sorry you were hurt."

He held her hand to him and smiled. "This is something I haven't shown to anyone else," he told her. "Except my brothers."

It made sense then. She looked up into his eyes. "A...lover's secret," she whispered, amazed that she could think of him like that, so easily.

He nodded. He wasn't smiling. "Like the freckles on your breasts, just around the nipples."

She felt her breath gathering speed, like an old-time steam engine. Her breasts felt tight, and not because of Sandy's rough handling. She frowned a little because it was uncomfortable and she still didn't quite understand it.

"We swell, both of us, when we're aroused," he said quietly, glancing at the small hand that had come up to rest a little gingerly against one taut nipple. "It's uncomfortable, isn't it?"

"Just...just a little." She felt like a child in a candy store, breathless with delight as she looked at him. "I liked...what you did," she whispered.

"So did I. Have a few sips of this and I'll do it again."

Her breath caught. She sipped and wrinkled her nose.

He took two more huge swallows before he put the can on the table and came back to her.

He stretched out beside her and this time when he slid his leg in between both of hers, it wasn't shocking or frightening. It felt natural, right. His hands slid under her as he bent again to her mouth. Now the kisses weren't tentative and seeking. They were slow and insistent and arousing. They were passionate kisses, meant to drag a response from the most unwilling partner.

Tess found herself clinging to him as if she might drown, her nails biting into his nape, and every kiss was more intimate than the last, more demanding, more arousing, more complete.

When his powerful body eased completely down over hers, she didn't protest at all. Her arms slid around his waist, her legs parted immediately, and she melted into the leather under them, welcoming the hard crush of him, the sudden heat and swelling that betrayed his hunger.

"You can feel it, can't you?" he whispered intimately at her ear and moved a little, just to make sure she could.

"Cag...!"

"I want you so badly, Tess!" he whispered, and his mouth slid over her cheek and onto her lips. He bit at them with a new and staggering intimacy that set her body on fire. When his tongue eased into her mouth, she opened her lips to accept it. When he pressed her legs further apart so that he could settle intimately between them, she arched into him. When he groaned and his hands found her breasts, she gave everything that she was into his keeping. He never thought he could draw back in time. He shook convulsively with the effort. He dragged his hips away and turned, lying on his back with Tess settled close against his side while he fought his own need, and hers.

"Don't...move!" he stated when she turned closer to him.

She stilled at once, half-heard bits of advice from a parade of motherly women coming back to her and making sudden sense.

She could feel Cag's powerful body vibrating with the hunger the kisses had built in it. He was like corded wood, breathing harshly. It fascinated her that he'd wanted her that much, when she was a rank beginner. He certainly wasn't!

When she felt him begin to relax, she let out a sigh of relief. She hadn't known what to do or say. Men in that condition were a mystery to her.

She felt his hand in her curly hair, holding her cheek to his chest. Under it, she heard the heavy, hard beat of his heart, like a fast drum.

"I haven't touched a woman since my fiancée threw me over," he said in a harsh tone.

Years ago. He didn't say it, but Tess knew that was what he was implying. She lifted her head and raised up, resting her hand on his shoulder to steady her as she searched his face. There was a hard flush along his high cheekbones, but his eyes were quiet, soft, full of mystery as they met hers.

"You want to know why I drew back."

She nodded.

He let go of her hair and touched her soft, swollen mouth with his. "You're a virgin."

He sounded so certain of it that she didn't bother to argue. It would have been pretty pointless at the moment, anyway.

"Oh. I see." She didn't, but it sounded mature.

He chuckled gently. "You don't know beans," he corrected. He moved suddenly, turning her over so that his body half covered hers and his eyes were inches from her own. His big hand caught her hip and curved it up into his intimately. The reaction of his body was fierce and immediate; and very stark. She flushed.

"I don't date anymore," he said, watching her mouth. "I don't have anything to do with women. This—" he moved her subtly against that part of him that was most obvious "—is delicious and heady and even a little shocking. I haven't felt it in a very long time."

Curiosity warred with embarrassment. "But I'm not experienced," she said.

He nodded. "And you think it should take an experienced woman to arouse me this much."

"Well, yes."

He bent and drew his lips over her open mouth in a shivery little caress that made her breath catch. "It happens every time I touch you," he whispered into her lips. "An experienced woman would have realized immediately why I was so hostile and antagonistic toward you. It's taken you months."

He covered her mouth with his, kissing her almost violently as his hand slid back inside her dress and played havoc with her self-control. But it only lasted seconds. He got up abruptly and pulled her up with him, holding her a few inches away from him with steely hands at her waist.

"You have to go to bed. Alone. Right now," he said emphatically.

Her breath came in soft spurts as she looked up at him with her heart in her eyes.

He actually groaned and pulled her close, into a bearish embrace. He stood holding her, shivering as they pressed together.

"Dear God," he whispered poignantly, and it sounded reverent, almost a plea for divine assistance. "Tess, do you know how old I am?'' he groaned at her ear. ''We're almost a generation apart!''

Her eyes were closed. She was dreaming. It had all been a dream, a sweet, sensuous dream that she never wanted to end.

''I can still feel your mouth on my breasts when I close my eyes,'' she whispered.

He made another rough sound and his arms tightened almost to pain. He didn't know how he was going to let her go.

''Baby,'' he whispered, ''this is getting dangerous.''

''You never called me 'baby' before,'' she murmured.

''I was never this close to being your lover before,'' he whispered gruffly. His head lifted and his black eyes glittered down into her pale blue ones. ''Not like this, Tess,'' he said roughly. ''Not in a fever, because you've had a bad experience.''

''You made love to me,'' she said, still dazed by the realization of how much their turbulent relationship had changed in the space of a few minutes.

''You wanted me to,'' he returned.

''Oh, yes,'' she confessed softly. Her lips parted and she watched, fascinated at the expression on his face when he looked down at them.

She reached up to him on tiptoe, amazed that it took such a tiny little tug to bring his hard mouth crashing passionately down onto her parted lips. He actually lifted her off the floor in his ardor, groaning as the kiss went on endlessly.

She felt swollen all over when he eased her back down onto her feet.

''This won't do,'' he said unsteadily. He held her by the shoulders, firmly. ''Are you listening?''

''I'm trying to,'' she agreed, searching his eyes as if

they held the key to paradise. His hands contracted. "I want you, honey," he said curtly. "Want you badly enough to seduce you, do you understand?" His gaze fell to her waist and lingered there with the beginnings of shock. All at once, he was thinking with real hunger of little boys with curly red hair...

Chapter Seven

"**W**hy are you looking at me like that?" Tess asked softly.

His hands contracted on her waist for an instant before he suddenly came to his senses and realized what he was thinking and how impossible it was. He closed his eyes and breathed slowly, until he got back the control he'd almost lost.

He put her away from him with an odd tenderness. "You're very young," he said. "I only meant to comfort you. Things just…got out of hand. I'm sorry."

She searched his eyes and knew that what they'd shared hadn't made a whit of difference to their turbulent relationship. He wanted her, all right, but there was guilt in his face. He thought she was too young for anything permanent. Or perhaps that was the excuse he had to use to conceal the real one—that he was afraid to get involved with a woman again because he'd been so badly hurt by one.

She dropped her gaze to his broad chest, watching its

jerky rise and fall curiously. He wasn't unaffected by her. That was oddly comforting.

"Thanks for getting rid of the bad memory, anyway," she said in a subdued tone.

He hesitated before he spoke, choosing his words. "Tess, it wasn't only that," he said softly. "But you have to realize how things are. I've been alone for a long time. I let you go to my head." He took a long, harsh breath. "I'm not a marrying man. Not anymore. But you're a marrying woman."

She ground her teeth together. Well, that was plain enough. She looked up at him, red-cheeked. "I didn't propose! And don't get your hopes up, because I won't. Ever. So there."

He cocked his head, and for an instant something twinkled deep in his eyes. "Never? I'm devastated."

The humor was unexpected and it eased the pain of the awkward situation a little. She peeked up at him. "You're very attractive," she continued, "but it takes more than looks to make a marriage. You can't cook and you don't know which end of a broom to use. Besides that, you throw cakes at people."

He couldn't deny that. His firm mouth, still swollen from the hot kisses they'd shared, tugged up at the corners. "I missed you by a mile. In fact," he reminded her, "you weren't even in the room when I threw it."

She held up a hand. "I'm sorry. It's too late for excuses. You're right off my list of marriage prospects. I hope you can stand the shock."

He chuckled softly. "So do I." She was still flushed, but she looked less tormented than she had. "Are you all right now?" he asked gently.

She nodded and then said, "Yes. Thank you," she added, her voice softer then she intended it to be.

He only smiled. "He won't be back, in case you're worried about that," he added. "I fired him on the spot."

She drew in a breath. "I can't say I'm sorry about that. He wasn't what he seemed."

"Most men aren't. And the next time you accept a date, I want to know first."

She stared at him. "I beg your pardon?"

"You heard me. You may not consider me good husband material," he murmured, "but I'm going to look out for your interests just the same." He studied her seriously for a moment. "If I can't seduce you, nobody else can, either."

"Well, talk about sour grapes!" she accused.

"Count on it," he agreed.

"And what if I want to be seduced?" she continued.

"Not this week," he returned dryly. "I'll have to look at my calendar."

"I didn't mean you!"

His black eyes slid up and down her body in the torn dress that she'd covered with his shirt. "You did earlier," he murmured with a tender smile. "And I wanted to."

She sighed. "So did I. But I won't propose, even if you beg."

He shrugged powerful shoulders. "My heart's broken."

She chuckled in spite of herself. "Sure it is."

She turned and reached for the doorknob.

"Tess."

She glanced back at him. "Yes?"

His face was solemn, no longer teasing. "They told you about her, didn't they?"

He meant his brothers had told her about his doomed engagement. She didn't pretend ignorance. "Yes, they did," she replied.

"It was a long time ago, but it took me years to get

over it. She was young, too, and she thought I was just what she wanted. But the minute I was out of sight, she found somebody else.''

"And you think I would, too, because I'm not mature enough to be serious,'' she guessed.

His broad chest rose and fell. "That's about the size of it. You're pretty green, honey. It might be nothing more concrete than a good case of repressed lust.''

"If that's my excuse, what's yours?'' she asked with pursed lips. "Abstinence?''

"That's my story and I'm sticking to it like glue.''

She laughed softly. "Coward.''

He lifted one eyebrow. "You can write a check on that. I've been burned and I've got the scars to prove it.''

"And I'm too young to be in love with you.''

His heart jerked in his chest. The thought of Tess being in love with him made his head spin, but he had to hold on to his common sense. "That's right.'' His gaze went homing to her soft mouth and he could taste it all over again. He folded his arms over his broad chest and looked at her openly, without amusement or mockery. "Years too young.''

"Okay. Just checking.'' She opened the door. A crash of thunder rumbled into the silence that followed. Seconds later, the bushes outside his window scratched against the glass as the wind raged.

"Are you afraid of storms?'' he asked.

She shook her head. "Are you?''

"I'll tell you tomorrow.''

She looked puzzled.

"You've spent enough time around livestock to know that thunderstorms play hell with cattle from time to time. We'll have to go out and check on ours if this keeps up.

You can lie in your nice, soft dry bed and think about all of us getting soaked to the skin.''

She thought about how bad summer colds could be. ''Wear a raincoat,'' she told him.

He smiled at that affectionate concern, and it was in his eyes this time, too. ''Okay, boss.''

She grinned. ''That'll be the day.''

He lifted an eyebrow. ''You're big on songs these days,'' he murmured. ''That was one of Buddy Holly's. Want me to sing it to you?''

She realized belatedly which song he was talking about, and she shook her head. ''No, thanks. It would upset the neighbors' dogs.''

He glowered at her. ''I have a good voice.''

''Sure you do, as long as you don't use it for singing,'' she agreed. ''Good night, Callaghan. Thanks again for rescuing me.''

''I can't let anything happen to the family biscuit chef,'' he said casually. ''We'd all starve.''

She let him get away with that. He might not believe in marriage, but he was different after their ardent interlude. He'd never picked at her, teased her, before. Come to think of it, she'd never teased him. She'd been too afraid. That was ancient history now. She gave him one last shy, smiling glance and went out the door.

He stood where she left him, his eyes narrowed, his body still singing with the pleasure she'd given him. She was too young. His mind knew it. If he could only convince the rest of him...

Surprisingly Tess slept that night, despite the storms that rippled by, one after another. The memory of Cag's tender passion had all but blotted out the bad memories Gaines had given her. If only Cag wanted her on a permanent basis. At least they'd gotten past the awkwardness that followed that physical explosion of pleasure. It would make things easier for both of them.

She made breakfast the following morning and there was nobody to eat it. One of the men, wet and bedraggled looking, came to the back door to explain why breakfast went untouched.

It seemed that the high winds combined with drenching rain had brought down some huge old oak trees, right through several fences. While she slept soundly, in the outer pastures, cattle had gotten loose and had to be rounded up again, and the broken fences had to be mended. Half the outfit was soaked and all but frozen from the effort. The brothers had dragged in about daylight and fallen asleep, too tired even for their beloved biscuits.

It was almost noon before they came wandering into the kitchen. Breakfast had gone to the ranch dogs and the chickens, but she had beef and potatoes in a thick stew—with biscuits—waiting.

Rey and Leo smiled at her. To her astonishment, Cag gave her an openly affectionate glance as he sat down at the head of the table and reached for the coffeepot.

"It amazes me how you always keep food hot," Leo remarked. "Thanks, Tess. We were dead on our feet when we finally got back this morning."

"It was a rough night, I gather," she murmured as she ferried butter and jam to the table.

Leo watched her curiously. "We heard that you had one of your own," he said, regretting the careless remark when he saw her flush. "I'm sorry we didn't get our hands on Gaines before he ran for the border," he added, and the familiar, funny man she'd come to know suddenly became someone else.

"That goes double for me," Rey added grimly.

"Well, he had plenty of attention without counting on either of you," Cag remarked pleasantly. "I understand that he left tire marks on his way out in the early hours of the morning. The sniveling little weasel," he added.

"Amazing, isn't it, that Gaines actually walked away under his own steam," Leo told Rey.

Rey nodded. "And here we've been wasting our time saving people from him—" he indicated Cag "—for years."

"People don't need saving from me," Cag offered. "I'm not a homicidal maniac. I can control my temper," he added.

Leo pursed his lips. "Say, Tess, did the chocolate icing stain ever come completely off the wall…?"

She was fumbling with a lid that wouldn't come off, flustered from the whole conversation and wishing she could sink through the floor.

"Here, give me that," Cag said softly.

She gave it to him. Their hands touched and they looked at each other for just a second too long, something the brothers picked up on immediately.

Cag opened the jar and put it on the table while she went to get spoons.

"At least he's stopped throwing cakes at people," Rey remarked.

Cag lifted the jar of apple butter and looked at his brother intently.

Rey held up a hand and grinned sheepishly as he fell to eating his stew.

"If it's all right, I thought I'd go ahead and apply to the local technical school," Tess said quickly, before she lost her nerve. "For fall classes in horticulture, you know."

"Sure," Leo said. "Go ahead."

Cag lifted his gaze to her slender body and remembered

how sweet it had been to hold in the silence of the study. He let his gaze fall back to his plate. He couldn't deter her. She didn't belong to him. She did need an occupation, something that would support her. He didn't like the idea of her keeping house for anyone else. She was safe here; she might not be in some other household. And if she went as a commuter, she could still work for the brothers.

"I could...live in the dormitory, if you want," she continued doggedly.

That brought Cag's head up. "Live in the dormitory? What the hell for?" he exclaimed.

His surprise took some of the gloom out of her heart. She clasped her hands tight in front of her, against her new jeans. "Well, you only said I could stay until summer," she said reasonably. "It's summer now. You didn't say anything about staying until fall."

Cag looked hunted. "You won't find another job easily in the fall, with all the high school seniors out grabbing them," he said curtly. He glanced back at his plate. "Stay until winter."

She wondered why Rey and Leo were strangling on their coffee.

"Is it too strong?" she asked worriedly, nodding toward the cups.

"Just...right." Leo chocked, coughing. "I think I caught cold last night. Sorry. I need a tissue..."

"Me, too!" Rey exploded.

They almost knocked over their chairs in their rush to get out of the room. Muffled laughter floated back even after the door had been closed.

"Idiots," Cag muttered. He looked up at Tess, and something brushed against his heart, as softly as a butterfly. He could hardly breathe.

She looked at him with eyes that loved him, and hated

the very feeling. He wanted her to go, she knew he did, but he kept putting it off because he was sorry for her. She was so tired of being pitied by him.

"I don't mind living in the dormitory at school, if you want me to leave here," she repeated softly.

He got up from his chair and moved toward her. His big, lean hands rested on her shoulders and he looked down from his great height with quiet, wondering eyes. She was already like part of him. She made him bubble inside, as if he'd had champagne. The touch of her, the taste of her, were suddenly all too familiar.

"How would you manage to support yourself, with no job?" he asked realistically.

"I could get something part-time, at the school."

"And who'll bake biscuits for us?" he asked softly. "And worry about us when we're tired? Who'll remember to set the alarm clocks and remind me to clean Herman's cage? Who'll fuss if I don't wear my raincoat?" he added affectionately.

She shrugged. His hands felt nice. She loved their warmth and strength, their tenderness.

He tilted her chin up and searched her quiet eyes. Fires kindled deep in his body and made him hungry. He couldn't afford to indulge what he was feeling. Especially not here, in the kitchen, where his brothers could walk in any minute.

But while he was thinking it, his rebellious hands slid up to frame her face and he bent, brushing his mouth tenderly over her soft lips.

"You shouldn't let me do this," he whispered.

"Oh, I'm not," she assured him softly. "I'm resisting you like crazy." She reached up to link her arms around his neck.

"Are you?" He smiled as he coaxed her lips under his and kissed her slowly.

She smiled against his mouth, lifting toward him. "Yes. I'm fighting like mad. Can't you tell?"

"I love the way you fight me...!"

The kiss became possessive, insistent, feverish, all in the space of seconds. He lifted her against him and groaned at the fierce passion she kindled in him so effortlessly.

Only the sound of booted feet heading their way broke them apart. He set her down gently and struggled to get back in his chair and breathe normally. He managed it, just.

Tess kept her back to the brothers until she could regain her own composure. But she didn't realize that her mouth was swollen and the softness in her eyes was an equally vivid giveaway.

Cag was cursing himself and circumstances under his breath for all he was worth. Having her here was going to be an unbearable temptation. Why hadn't he agreed to letting her live in at the school?

Because he ached for her, that was why. He was alive as he hadn't been in seven long years and the thought of going back into his shell was painful.

His black eyes settled on Tess and he wondered how he could ever have lived from day to day without looking at her at least once. He was getting a fixation on red curly hair and pale freckled skin. She was too young for him. He knew that, but he couldn't seem to keep his hands off her. He didn't know what he was going to do. If he didn't find something to occupy him, and quickly, he was going to end up seducing her. That would be the end of the world. The absolute end.

Tess borrowed one of the ranch trucks the next morning after breakfast and drove herself to the campus of the Jacobsville Vocational-Technical School. The admissions office was easy to find. She was given forms to fill out, a course schedule for the fall quarter, and advice on financial assistance. From there, she went to the financial office and filled out more forms. It took until lunch to finally finish, but she had a sense of accomplishment by the time she left the campus.

On her way back to the ranch, she stopped in at the local café and had coffee and a sandwich while she did some thinking about her situation.

Cag said he didn't want her to move out, but did he really mean it, or was he just sorry for her? He liked kissing her, but he didn't want to keep doing it. He seemed not to be able to stop. Maybe, she thought, that was the whole problem. She made him forget all the reasons why he shouldn't get involved with her, every time he came close.

If she was gone, of course, he wouldn't get close enough to have his scruples damaged. But he'd said that he didn't want her to leave. It was a puzzle she couldn't seem to solve.

The sandwich tasted flat, although it was roast beef, one of her favorites. She put it down and stared at it without seeing.

"Thinking of giving it its freedom, huh?" Leo asked with a grin, and sat down across from her. He took off his hat, laid it on the chair beside him and gestured toward the sandwich. "I hate to tell you this, but there's absolutely no way known to science that a roast beef sandwich can be rejuvenated." He leaned forward conspiratorially. "Take it from a beef expert."

She chuckled despite her sadness. "Oh, Leo, you're just impossible," she choked.

"It runs in the family." He held up a hand and when the waitress came to see what he wanted, he ordered coffee.

"No lunch?" Tess asked.

He shook his head. "No time. I'm due at the Brewsters's in forty-five minutes for a business meeting over lunch. Rubber chicken and overdone potatoes, like last time," he muttered. He glanced at her. "I wish you were cooking for it instead of Brewster's daughter. She's pretty as a picture and I hear tell she had operatic aspirations, but she couldn't make canned soup taste good."

He sounded so disgusted that Tess smiled in spite of herself. "Are you going by yourself, or are the brothers going, too?"

"Just Cag and me. Rey escaped on a morning flight to Tulsa to close a land deal up there."

She lowered her eyes to the half-finished sandwich. "Does Cag like her...Miss Brewster?"

He hesitated. "Cag doesn't like women, period. I thought you knew."

"You said she was pretty."

"Like half a dozen other women who have fathers in the cattle business," he agreed. "Some of them can even cook. But as you know Cag gave up on women when he was thrown over for a younger man. Hell, the guy was only three years younger than him, at that. She used his age as an excuse. It wasn't, really. She just didn't want him. The other guy had money, too, and she did want him."

"I see."

He sipped coffee and pursed his lips thoughtfully. "I've told you before how Cag reacts to women most of the time," he reminded her. "He runs." He smiled. "Of course, he's been doing his best to run from you since last Christmas.''

She looked at him with her heart in her eyes. "He has?" she asked.

"Sure! He wants you to go off to school so you'll remove temptation from his path. But he also wants you to stay at the ranch while you go to school, in case you run into any handsome eligible bachelors there. I think he plans to save you from them, if you do."

She was confused and it showed.

"He said," he related, "that you shouldn't be exposed to potential seducers without us to protect you."

She didn't know whether to laugh or cry.

He held up a hand when she started to speak. "He thinks you should commute."

"But he doesn't want me at the ranch, don't you see?" she asked miserably, running a hand through her short, curly hair. "He keeps leaving to get away from me!"

"Why would he leave if you weren't getting to him?" he asked reasonably.

"It's still a rotten way to live," she said pointedly. "Maybe if I go to school I'll meet somebody who'll think I'm old enough for them."

"Oh, that's just sour grapes," he murmured dryly.

"You have no idea *how* sour," she replied. "I give up. I can't spend the rest of my life hoping that he'll change his mind about me. He's had almost a year, and he hasn't changed a thing."

"He stopped throwing cakes," he said.

"Because I stopped baking them!"

He checked his watch and grimaced. "I'd love to stay here and talk recipes with you, but I'm late." He got up and smiled at her. "Don't brood, okay? I have a feeling that things are going to work out just fine."

That wasn't what she thought, but he was gone before she could put the thought into words.

Chapter Eight

It was inevitable that Leo would bring up the matter of the Brewster girl's cooking the next day. Breakfast was too much of a rush, and they didn't get to come home for lunch. But when two of the three brothers and Tess sat down to supper, Leo let it fly with both barrels.

"That Janie Brewster isn't too bad-looking, is she?" Leo murmured between bites of perfectly cooked barbecued chicken. "Of course, she can ruin a chicken."

Cag glanced at him quickly, as if the remark puzzled him. Then he glanced at Tess's studiously downbent head and understood immediately what Leo was trying to do.

He took a forkful of chicken and ate it before he replied, "She'll never make a cook. Or even much of a wife," he added deliberately. "She knows everything."

"She does have a university degree."

"In psychology," Cag reminded him. "I got psychoanalyzed over every bite of food." He glanced at Tess. "It seems that I have repressed feelings of inadequacy because

I keep a giant reptile,'' he related with a twinkle in his black eyes.

Tess's own eyes widened. "You do?"

He nodded. "And I won't eat carrots because I have some deep-seated need to defy my mother."

She put a napkin to her mouth, trying to ward off laughter.

"You forgot the remark she made about the asparagus," Leo prompted.

Cag looked uncomfortable. "We can forget that one."

"But it's the best one!" Leo turned to Tess. "She said that he won't eat asparagus because of associations with impo—"

"Shut up!" Cag roared.

Leo, who never meant to repeat the blatant sexual remark, only grinned. "Okay."

Tess guessed, quite correctly, that the word Cag had cut off was "impotence." And she was in a perfect position to tell Leo that it certainly didn't apply to his older brother, but she wouldn't have dared.

As it was, her eyes met Cag's across the table, and she flushed at the absolutely wicked glitter in those black eyes, and almost upset her coffee.

Leo, watching the byplay, was affectionately amused at the two of them trying so hard not to react. There was a sort of intimate merriment between them, despite Cag's attempts to ward off intimacy. Apparently he hadn't been wholly successful.

"I've got a week's worth of paperwork to get through," Cag said after a minute, getting up.

"But I made dessert," Tess said.

He turned, surprised. "I don't eat sweets. You know that."

She smiled secretively. "You'll like this one. It isn't really a conventional dessert."

He pushed in his chair. "Okay," he said. "But you'll have to bring it to me in the office. How about some coffee, too?"

"Sure."

Leo put down his napkin. "Well, you do the hard stuff. I'm going down to Shea's Bar to see if I can find Billy Telford. He promised me faithfully that he was going to give me a price on that Salers bull we're after. He's holding us up hoping that he can get more from the Tremaynes."

"The Tremaynes don't run Salers cattle," Cag said, frowning.

"Yes, but that's because Billy's only just been deluging them with facts on the advantages of diversification." He shrugged. "I don't think they'll buy it, but Billy does. I'm going to see if I can't get him dru...I mean," he amended immediately, "get him to give me a price."

"Don't you dare," Cag warned. "I'm not bailing you out again. I mean it."

"You drink from time to time," Leo said indignantly.

"With good reason, and I'm quiet about it. You aren't. None of us have forgotten the last time you cut loose in Jacobsville."

"I'd just gotten my degree," Leo said curtly. "It was a great reason to celebrate."

"To celebrate, yes. Not to wreck the bar. And several customers."

"As I recall, Corrigan and Rey helped."

"You bad boys," Tess murmured under her breath.

Cag glanced at her. "I never drink to excess anymore."

"Neither do I. And I didn't say that I was going to get

drunk," Leo persisted. "I said I was going to get *Billy* drunk. He's much more malleable when he's not sober."

Cag shook a finger at him. "Nothing he signs inebriated will be legal. You remember that."

Leo threw up both hands. "For heaven's sake!"

"We can do without that bull."

"We can't! He's a grand champion," Leo said with pure, naked hunger in his tone. "I never saw such a beautiful animal. He's lean and healthy and glossy, like silk. He's a sire worthy of a foundation herd. I want him!"

Cag exchanged an amused glance with Tess. "It's love, I reckon," he drawled.

"With all due respect to women," Leo sighed, "there is nothing in the world more beautiful than a pedigree bull in his prime."

"No wonder you aren't married, you pervert," Cag said.

Leo glared at him. "I don't want to marry the bull, I just want to own him! Listen, your breeding program is standing still. I have ideas. Good ideas. But I need that bull." He slammed his hat down on his head. "And one way or another, Billy's going to sell him to me!"

He turned and strode out the door, looking formidable and determined.

"Is it really that good a bull?" Tess asked.

Cag chuckled. "I suppose it is." He shook his head. "But I think Leo has ulterior motives."

"Such as?"

"Never you mind." He studied her warmly for a minute, approving of her chambray shirt and jeans. She always looked neat and feminine, even if she didn't go in for seductive dresses and tight-fitting clothes. "Bring your mysterious dessert on into the office when you get it ready. Don't forget the coffee."

"Not me, boss," she replied with a pert smile.

* * *

She put the finishing touches on the elegant dessert and placed it on a tray with the cup of coffee Cag liked after supper. She carried the whole caboodle into the study, where he was hunched over his desk with a pencil in one hand and his head in the other, going over what looked like reams of figure-studded pages of paper.

He got up when she entered and took the tray from her, placing it on the very edge of the desk. He scowled.

"What is it?" he asked, nodding toward a saucer of what looked like white foam rubber with whipped cream on top.

"It's a miniature Pavlova," she explained. "It's a hard meringue with a soft center, filled with fresh fruit and whipped cream. It takes a long time to make, but it's pretty good. At least, I think it is."

He picked up the dessert fork she'd provided and drew it down through the dessert. It made a faint crunching sound. Intrigued, he lifted a forkful of the frothy-looking substance to his mouth and tasted it. It melted on his tongue.

His face softened. "Why, this is good," he said, surprised.

"I thought you might like it," she said, beaming. "It isn't really a sweet dessert. It's like eating a cloud."

He chuckled. "That's a pretty good description." He sat down in the big leather swivel chair behind his desk with the saucer in his hand. But he didn't start eating again.

He lifted his chin. "Come here."

"Who, me?" she asked.

"Yes, you."

She edged closer. "You said that I mustn't let you do things to me."

"Did I say that?" he asked in mock surprise.

"Yes, you did."

He held out the arm that wasn't holding the saucer. "Well, ignore me. I'm sure I was out of my mind at the time."

She chuckled softly, moving to the chair. He pulled her down onto his lap so that she rested against his broad chest, with his shoulder supporting her back. He dipped out a forkful of her dessert and held it to her lips.

"It's not bad, is it?" she asked, smiling.

He took a bite of his own. "It's unique. I'll bet the others would love it, too." He glanced down at her expression and lifted an eyebrow. "Mm-hmm," he murmured thoughtfully. "So you made it just for me, did you?"

She shifted closer. "You work harder than everybody else. I thought you deserved something special."

He smiled warmly at her. "I'm not the only hard worker around here. Who scrubbed the kitchen floor on her hands and knees after I bought her a machine that does it?"

She flushed. "It's a very nice machine. I really appreciate it. But it's better if you do it with a toothbrush. I mean, the dirt in the linoleum pattern just doesn't come up any other way. And I do like a nice kitchen."

He grimaced. "What am I going to do with you? A modern woman isn't supposed to scrub floors on her hands and knees. She's supposed to get a degree and take a corporate presidency away from some good old boy in Houston."

She snuggled close to him and closed her eyes, loving his warm strength against her. Her hand smoothed over his shirt just at the pocket, feeling its softness.

"I don't want a degree. I'd like to grow roses."

"So you said." He fed her another bite of the dessert,

which left one for himself. Then he sat up to put the saucer on the desk and reach for the coffee.

"I'll get it." She slid off his lap and fixed the coffee the way he liked it.

He took it from her and coaxed her back onto his lap. It felt good to hold her like that, in the pleasant silence of the office. He shared the coffee with her, too.

Her hand rested on his while she sipped the hot liquid, staring up into eyes that seemed fascinated by her. She wondered at their sudden closeness, when they'd been at odds for such a long time.

He was feeling something similar. He liked holding her, touching her. She filled an empty place in him with joy and delight. He wasn't lonely when she was close to him.

"Why roses?" he asked when they finished the coffee and he put the cup back on the desk.

"They're old," she said, settling back down against his chest. "They have a nobility, a history. For instance, did you know that Napoleon's Empress Josephine was famous for her rose garden, and that despite the war with England, she managed to get her roses shipped through enemy lines?"

He chuckled. "Now how did you know about that?"

"It was in one of my gardening magazines. Roses are prehistoric," she continued. "They're one of the oldest living plants. I like the hybrids, too, though. Dad bought me a beautiful tea rose the last year we lived in Victoria. I guess it's still where I planted it. But the house was rented, and we weren't likely to have a permanent home after that, so I didn't want to uproot my rosebush."

He smoothed his fingers over her small, soft hand where it pressed over his pocket. His fingers explored her neat, short nails while his breath sighed out at her forehead, ruffling her hair.

"I never had much use for flowers. Our mother wasn't much of a gardener, either."

She leaned back against his shoulder so that she could see his face. He looked bitter.

Her fingers went up to his mouth and traced his hard, firm lips. "You mustn't try to live in the past," she said. "There's a whole world out there waiting to be seen and touched and lived in."

"How can you be so optimistic, after the life you've had?" he wanted to know.

"I'm an incurable optimist, I guess," she said. "I've seen so much of the ugly side of life that I never take any nice thing for granted. It's been great, living here, being part of a family, even though I just work for you."

His lips pursed against her exploring fingers. He caught them and nibbled absently at their tips while he looked down into her eyes. "I like the way you cook."

"I'm not pretty, though," she mused, "and I can't psychoanalyze you over the vegetables."

"Thank God."

She chuckled.

He tugged at a lock of her hair and searched her eyes. "Cute of Leo to bring up the asparagus." His eyes narrowed and his smile faded as he looked down at her with kindling desire. "You knew what he was going to say, didn't you?"

She nodded. Her heart was racing too fast to allow for speech.

"Well, it was interesting, having asparagus signify impotence," he murmured dryly, smiling at her blush. "But we could have told Miss Brewster that the asparagus lied, couldn't we, Tess?" he drawled.

She hid her hot face against him, feeling his laughter as his chest rippled with it.

"Sorry," he said at her ear, bending to gather her even closer against him. "I shouldn't tease you. It's irresistible. I love the way you blush." His arms tightened and his face nuzzled against hers, coaxing it around so that his lips could find her soft mouth. "I love...so much about you, Tess," he growled against her lips.

She reached up to hold him while the kiss grew and grew, like a spark being fanned into a bonfire.

He lifted away from her for an instant, to search her eyes and look down at her soft, yielding body.

Without the slightest hesitation, his hand smoothed over the chambray shirt she was wearing and went right to her small breast, covering it boldly, teasing the nipple to immediate hardness with his thumb.

Her lips parted with the excitement he aroused, and he bent and took her soft sigh right into his mouth.

She didn't have the experience to know how rare this mutual delight was, but he did. It was pleasurable with some women, but with Tess, it was like walking through fireworks. He enjoyed every single thing about her, from the way she curled into him when he touched her to the way her mouth opened eagerly for his. It made him feel vaguely invincible.

He made a rough sound in his throat as his hand edged between them, feeling blindly for her shirt buttons. She wasn't coy about that, either. She lay submissively in his arms, letting him open the shirt, letting him unclip her bra and push it away.

She didn't have to tell him that she liked his gazing on her body. It was even in the way her breath caught and fluttered.

He touched her delicately, lifting his gaze to her face to watch the way she reacted to it.

It occurred to him that she might love him, must love

him, to let him be so familiar with her body, which he knew instinctively was innocent.

His heart jumped up into his throat as he traced around one tight little pink nipple.

"What did you do for experience before I came along?" he murmured half-teasingly.

"I watched movies on cable," she said, her own voice breathless. She shivered and her short nails dug into his shoulder. "Callaghan, is it supposed to...do that?" she whispered.

"What?"

She bit her lip and couldn't quite look at him.

He bent to her mouth and liberated her lower lip with a soft, searching kiss. "It's supposed to make your body swell," he whispered into her lips. "Does it?"

She swallowed hard. "All over?"

"All over."

She nuzzled her face into his hot throat while his hands worked magic on her. "It makes me ache."

"It's supposed to do that, too."

He had the weight of her in one big palm and he bent his head to put his mouth, open, on the nipple.

She shivered again and he heard a tight sob pass her lips. He knew he was going to get in over his head, and it didn't seem to matter anymore.

With a rough curse, he suddenly got to his feet and stripped her out of the shirt and bra before he lifted her and, with his mouth hard on hers, carried her to the divan.

He stretched her out on it, yielding and openly hungry, and came down beside her, one long leg inserted boldly between both of hers.

"Do you have any idea how dangerous this is?" he ground out against her breasts.

Her hands were fumbling for buttons. "It isn't, because

we aren't…doing anything,'' she whispered with deathbed humor as she forced the stubborn shirt buttons apart and pushed the fabric away from hard, warm, hair-covered muscles. ''You are…so beautiful,'' she added in a hushed, rapt whisper as she touched him and felt him go tense.

His teeth clenched. ''Tess…'' He made her name sound like a plea for mercy.

''Oh, come here. Please!'' She drew him down on her, so that her bare breasts merged with his hard chest. She held him close while they kissed hungrily, feeling his long legs suddenly shift so that he was between them, pressing against her in a new and urgent way.

He lifted his head and looked into her eyes. His own were coal black, glittering with desire, his face drawn and taut.

She watched him openly, all too aware of his capability, and that he could lose his head right here and she wouldn't care.

He shifted against her deliberately, and his head spun with pleasure. He laughed, but without humor.

''If I'd ever imagined that a virgin—'' he stressed the word in a harsh, choked tone ''—could make an utter fool of me!''

Her hands had been sliding up and down the hard muscles of his back with pure wonder. Now they stilled, uncertain. ''A…fool?'' she whispered.

''Tess, have you gone numb from the waist down?'' he asked through his teeth. ''Can't you feel what's happened to me?''

''Well…yes,'' she said hesitantly. ''Isn't it normal?''

He laughed in spite of the stabbing ache she'd given him. ''Baby, you haven't got a clue, have you?''

''Did I do something wrong?''

''No!'' He eased down again, giving in to his need, and

hers, but careful not to give her too much of his formidable weight. His mouth moved lazily over her forehead, down to close her wide, wounded eyes. "You haven't done anything wrong. I want you," he whispered tenderly.

"I want you, too," she whispered back shyly.

He sighed as if he had the weight of the world on him. One big, lean hand slid under her hips and lifted them slowly, sensually into the hard thrust of him, and held her there.

She stiffened suddenly and a tiny little cry crawled out of her tight throat as she registered the heat and power of him in such stark intimacy.

"When it gets this bad," he whispered at her ear, "a man will lie, cheat, steal, kill to get rid of it! If I had just a little less honor, I'd tell you anything that would get those jeans off you in the least possible time."

"Get my jeans off…!"

The shock in her voice broke the tension. He lifted his head and burst out laughing despite the urgency in his body when he saw her face.

"You don't imagine that we could make love *through* them?" he asked.

She was scarlet. And he was laughing, the animal! She hit his shoulder angrily. "You stop that!"

He chuckled helplessly, shifting suddenly to lie beside her on the wide leather divan. He pulled her against him and lay there fighting for breath and control, deliciously aware of her bare breasts pressing warmly against his rib cage.

"Just when I think I'll go mad, you act your age."

"I'm not a kid!" she protested.

He smoothed her ruffled hair lazily and his chest rose and fell in a long sigh while the urgency slowly passed out of his body. "Yes, you are," he contradicted, his voice soft and affectionate. "And if we keep doing this, eventually, blushes or not, you're coming out of those jeans."

"As if I'd let you!"

"You'd help me," he returned. "Tess, I haven't really tried to seduce you," he added quietly. "You're as hungry for me as I am for you, and I know tricks I haven't used yet."

She drank in the male smell of his body with pleasure. "Such as?"

"You really want to know?" He drew her close and whispered in her ear.

"Callaghan!"

He kissed her shocked face, closing her open mouth with warm, tender kisses. "You've got a lot to learn, and I ache to teach it to you," he said after a minute. "But you aren't geared for an affair, and I have far too many principles to seduce a woman who works for me." He sighed wearily and drew her closer, wrapping her up against him. "Good God, Tess, how did we ever get into this situation?"

"You insisted that I sit on your lap while you ate dessert," she replied reasonably.

"It happened long before that. Months ago. I fought you like mad to keep you at arm's length."

"It didn't work," she informed him.

"So I noticed."

He didn't speak again and neither did she for a long time. They lay in each others' arms in the silence of the study, listening to the muted sounds of the night outside the window.

"Do you want me to go?" she asked finally.

His arms contracted. "Sure," he replied facetiously. "Like I want to give up breathing."

That was reassuring. She felt the same way. But he still

wasn't mentioning anything permanent. Even through the euphoria of lying half nude against him, she did realize that.

Finally he let go of her and got up from the divan, careful not to look at her as he fetched her shirt and bra and put them beside her.

"You'd better…" He gestured, not putting it into words.

She dressed quickly, watching his long back as he stood beside the desk, idly touching the papers on it.

She got to her feet at last and after a minute she went around him to get the tray.

"I'll take this back to the kitchen."

He nodded without speaking. He was too choked with conflicting emotions to put a single one of them into words.

But when she went to pick up the tray, his hand covered the back of hers, briefly.

"I've put off a conference that I meant to attend in Kansas City," he said quietly. "I'm going to go. Rey will be back in the morning before I leave, and Leo will be here."

She looked up at him with wide, soft eyes in a face that made his heart ache.

He cursed softly. "Tess, it wouldn't work," he said through his teeth. "You know it wouldn't!"

She made a motion with her shoulders and lowered her revealing eyes so that he couldn't read what was in them. "Okay."

"You'll like school," he forced himself to say. "There will be boys your own age, nice boys, not like some of the toughs you meet on the rodeo circuit."

"Sure."

"You can commute," he added after a minute. "None

of us want you to give up your job while you're going to school. And I'll make sure we aren't alone again, like this.''

She swallowed the lump in her throat and even forced a smile. "Okay."

He watched her pick up the tray and go out of the room. When he finally closed the door behind her, it was like putting the finishing touches on a high wall. He actually winced.

Chapter Nine

Cag was dressed in a lightweight gray vested suit the next morning when he came in to breakfast. His suitcase was packed and waiting by the front door, along with his silver belly Stetson. He looked elegant when he dressed up. Tess had to force herself not to stare at him too closely while she served the meal.

Rey had walked in, still dressed in a suit himself, just as Tess started to put breakfast down on the table. He, like Callaghan, would never win any beauty contests, but he paid for dressing. He looked elegant and faintly dangerous, in a sexy sort of way. Tess was glad she was immune to him, and wondered vaguely if there had ever been a special woman in his life.

"I feel like Cinderella before the ball," Leo muttered, glancing from one of his brothers to the other. He was in jeans and a blue-checked shirt and boots, his blond-streaked brown hair shining like gold in the ceiling light.

Cag didn't react, but Rey took him up on it, peering

deliberately under the table to see if Leo was wearing a dress.

"Cute, cute," Leo drawled. He picked up his fork and stabbed the air toward his brother. "I meant figuratively speaking. I don't wear dresses."

"Good thing, with your hairy legs," Rey retorted. He glanced toward Cag. "You leaving?"

Cag nodded as he finished a mouthful of eggs and washed it down with coffee. "I'm going to that legislative cattlemen's conference in Kansas City. I decided that I'd better go. The journals don't keep us completely up-to-date on pending legislation, and I've heard some rumors I don't like about new regulations."

"I've heard those same rumors," Leo remarked.

"We have to start policing our own industry better," Cag said. "All the rules and regulations and laws in the world won't work without better enforcement." He looked up. "You should have kept your seat on the legislative committee at the state cattlemen's association."

"Hindsight is a fine thing," Leo agreed. "I had too much to do at the time."

"If they ask you again, take it."

"You bet I will." He glanced at Cag. "Why don't you do it?"

Cag smiled. "I've got more than I can do already, as you'll discover when you look at the paperwork in the study. I only got half the figures keyed into the computer. You'll need to take the rest down to Margie in the office and get her to finish."

"Sure."

Neither Leo nor Rey noticed that Tess had turned away to the sink deliberately, because she knew why Cag hadn't finished that paperwork. She didn't want the other two brothers to see her flush.

Cag noticed. He didn't look at her, though, because he'd become more readable lately where she was concerned. He finished his coffee and got up.

"Well, I'm off. I'll try to be back by next weekend. You can reach me at the Airport Hilton in Kansas City if you need me."

"We won't," Leo said with a grin. "Have a good time."

Cag glanced involuntarily at Tess, thinking how empty life without her was going to be, even for a few days. He'd grown all too fond of that red curly head of hair and those heavenly blue eyes.

"Take care of Tess while I'm gone," he said, trying to make a joke of it and failing miserably.

"I'll take care of myself, thanks very much," she shot right back and forced a smile, so that he'd think it wasn't killing her to watch him walk out the door.

"You never told us how your application went," Leo said suddenly.

"Oh, I was accepted on the spot," Tess said. "They've scheduled me for three classes when fall quarter begins. I went to the financial aid office and applied for tuition, which they say I can get, and it will pay for my books."

Cag frowned. "You've already applied?"

"Yes," she said with determined brightness. "I start in three weeks. I can hardly wait."

"So I see." Cag finished his goodbyes, added a few things for his brothers to take care of while he was away and left without another word.

Tess wondered why he was irritated that she'd applied for admission to the vocational school, when he'd already said he wanted her to do it. She knew he hadn't changed his mind. His behavior was puzzling.

Cag was thinking the same thing as he slammed his hat

on his head, picked up his suitcase, and went out the front door. He'd known she was applying, but now it was definite. He thought of her in his arms the night before, hungry for his kisses, and then he thought of all the young men she'd meet when she started classes. She might meet a young man who liked roses, too. He had visions of her youthful crush on him melting quickly away in the heat of a new romance, and it made him vaguely sick.

He'd tried not to get in over his head, but it looked as if he was only fooling himself. Tess had wormed her way under his skin, right where his heart was. He wondered how he'd ever imagined that he could make a little love to her and walk away. He'd never been quite so confused or worried in his life. He wanted Tess as he'd never wanted anything. But he was afraid that she was in love with love, not him, because he was the first man who'd ever been intimate with her even in a slight way. He couldn't forget the fiancée who'd dropped him for someone younger. He couldn't bear to go through that a second time.

He got into the ranch truck and drove toward the airport, but his heart wasn't in it. Tess was going to go away to school, and he was going to lose her. But not right away, he comforted himself. She'd still be living at the ranch. He'd have time to get himself sorted out. And it wasn't as if she was going to meet someone else at once. He had plenty of time. The thought comforted him, and he put that worry aside.

Cag wouldn't have been quite so comforted if he'd seen the big black limousine that drew up in front of the Hart ranch house barely two hours after he'd left.

Rey and Leo had already gone out with the men to look over a new batch of bulls when someone rang the doorbell.

Tess wiped her hands on a kitchen towel and left the pots she'd been scrubbing in the sink when she went to answer it.

A tall, taciturn man in a suit, carrying a briefcase, was standing there.

"Miss Theresa Brady?" the man asked politely.

It was a shock to hear her given name. She'd been called Tess for so long that she'd all but forgotten that it was a contraction of Theresa.

"Yes," she said hesitantly.

He held out a hand. "I'm Clint Matherson," he said, shaking hands. "Your late mother's attorney."

Her hand went limp in his. "My... *late*... mother?"

"I'm sorry to tell you that your mother passed away almost a month ago in Singapore. It wasn't possible to get word to you until now. I found you through a detective agency, but I've been out of town and the message only reached me a week ago. I'm very sorry," he said belatedly.

She hadn't thought of her mother in years, and only then with regret. It might have been sad to lose her if she'd ever shown the slightest affection for her only child, but she hadn't.

"I didn't know where she was," Tess said honestly. "We hadn't communicated since I was sixteen."

"Yes, she, uh, made me aware of that. She left you a portfolio of stocks in a trading company out of Singapore," he added. "If we could sit down and discuss her will?"

"I'm sorry. Of course. Come into the living room, please."

He sat down in an armchair and laid out the documents on the spotless oak coffee table, moving her flower arrangement aside to make room for them.

"I can't tell you much about this company. Frankly the

stocks are as much a surprise to you as they are to me. She didn't ask my advice before she sank her money into them. You did know that she married a wealthy Singapore importer six years ago?''

"No," Tess said stiffly. "As I said, we haven't corresponded."

"A pity," he replied. "She gave up drinking and led a fairly admirable life in her last years. She was widowed about the time she contracted cancer. Her illness perhaps changed her outlook somewhat. I understand that she had plans to ask you to come out and visit with her, but she never carried them out." He smiled thinly. "She told me she was ashamed of the way she'd treated you, Miss Brady, and not too hopeful of making amends."

Tess clasped her hands together on the knees of her jeans. "I would have listened, if she'd wanted to talk to me."

He shrugged. "Perhaps it's just as well. But time is a great healer." He indicated the documents. "I'll have these stocks checked out by the end of the week. I should be able to give you some idea of their current worth on the Asian market then. You can decide whether you'd rather keep them or sell them. There are a few odds and ends, like her jewelry, which will be sent on to me and I'll forward them to you."

The thought of having something, anything, of her mother's made her uneasy. "Wasn't there any other relative?"

"A stepdaughter who still lives in Singapore. But she was already provided for by her father's will."

"Wouldn't she like the jewelry?"

He was surprised. "Well, she was fond of your mother, I understand. They were good friends. Yes, I imagine she would like it. But it's yours, Miss Brady. You were a blood relative.''

''I never felt like one,'' she replied stiffly. ''I'd like the daughter to have the jewelry and the other...personal things.'' She glanced at him and away. ''It's hard to put into words, but I don't really want anything of hers. Not even the stock.''

''Ah, but you have no choice about that,'' he said, surprising her. ''There's no provision if you don't accept it. There must be some goal you've set in life that it would help you achieve. I understand that you work as a housekeeper here since your father's untimely death. Wouldn't you like to be financially independent?''

That remark changed her life. If she had a little money of her own, Callaghan wouldn't have to keep her on here because he was sorry for her. It would give her some measure of independence, even if leaving Callaghan broke her heart.

''Yes, I would,'' she answered the lawyer. ''And I'll accept the stock. Thank you.''

He indicated the places her signature was required, closed the documents up in his briefcase, shook hands and promised to be in touch soon about the stock.

''How much do you think it could be worth?'' she asked hesitantly when he was on the verge of leaving.

''Hard to tell. It was bought for eighty dollars a share, but that was last year.''

''And how much was bought?''

He smiled musingly. ''About a million dollars worth.''

She was pale. Her hand found the door and held on for support. ''Oh.''

''So you see, you won't be dependent on other people for your livelihood. Your mother may have neglected you in life, but she didn't forget you at the end. That must be some comfort."

It wasn't, but she smiled and pretended that it was. She closed the door and leaned back against it. Everything had changed in the course of a few minutes. She was a woman of means. She could do what she pleased. But it would be without Callaghan Hart, and that was the hardest pill of all to swallow.

She told the brothers about her visitor at the supper table.

They were silent after she related the size of the inheritance, glancing at each other as if communicating in some mysterious fashion.

"I can still go to school, but I'll be able to support myself now," she told them. "And I guess," she added reluctantly, "I won't need to work. I'm sorry to leave, but we've known for a long time that Callaghan really would prefer to have another cook."

"Why don't you ever call him Cag, like we do?" Leo asked gently.

She stared at her coffee cup. "It never seemed comfortable, I guess."

They exchanged another mysterious glance.

"Well, we'll advertise as soon as Cag comes home and we have time to discuss what we want to do," Rey said. "We'll miss you, Tess. Especially your biscuits."

"Amen to that. A good biscuit chef is really hard to find in these liberated times. I guess we'll be eating them out of tins from now on."

"Now, now," Tess chided, "Dorie can bake biscuits and even real bread. I'll bet she won't mind keeping you supplied. But you'll find a cook. I know you will."

They looked at her silently. "She won't be you," Leo said, and he smiled wistfully.

* * *

Tess got used to the idea of leaving in the days that followed. She was almost reconciled to it when Cag showed up late the next Friday afternoon. He looked tired and worn and unhappy until he saw Tess. His black eyes began to light up at once, and her heart ached, because it could have been so different if he'd loved her. She stood quietly in the kitchen when she wanted to fling herself into his arms and kiss him to death.

"Missed me?" he drawled.

She nodded, but she wouldn't look at him. "I've got to gather eggs. I forgot this morning. Welcome home," she said belatedly as she carried a small wicker basket out the back door.

"There you are!" Leo called, joining his brother in the kitchen. He clapped a hand on the taller man's shoulder. "How'd it go?"

"Fine. What's wrong with Tess?"

"What do you mean?"

Cag's eyes darkened. "She wouldn't look at me."

"Oh. Well, she's been unsettled since the lawyer came," Leo replied, carefully choosing his words. "Sudden wealth would do that to most people."

Cag's face lost a few shades of color. "Wealth?"

"Her mother died and left her a small fortune in stocks," he told the older man, watching with compassion the effect it had on him. "She says she'll be leaving as soon as we can hire a replacement. No need for her to work with a million dollars worth of stock, is there?"

Cag went to the sink and poured himself a glass of water that he didn't want, just to keep from groaning aloud. Tess had money. She was quitting. He'd thought he had time to work out his own feelings, and suddenly it was all up. She was leaving and he'd never see her again. She'd find somebody younger and get married and have babies. Tess would love having children of her own....

He put the glass down with a thud. "I've got things to do. How about those new bulls?"

"They came in, and I got Billy to sell me that Salers bull," he added smugly. "I've put him in a pasture all to himself with his own salt lick and a nice clean stall to keep him out of bad weather when it comes."

Cag didn't rise to the occasion which he would have only days before. He looked thoughtful and worried. Very worried.

"It won't be the same without Tess, will it?" Leo prompted gently.

Cag's face closed up completely. "I'll change and get back to the paperwork."

"Aren't you going to tell me how the conference went?"

"Later," Cag said absently. He walked out of the room without a backward glance.

He acted oddly for the rest of the day. And he wasn't at the supper table.

"Said he had to go into town, God knows what for," Rey murmured as he buttered a flaky biscuit. "They pull in the sidewalks at six. He knows that."

"Maybe he's got something on his mind," Leo mused, watching Tess fuss over the chicken dish she was putting into a serving bowl.

Rey sighed. "Something big. He wasn't going toward Jacobsville," he added. "He was headed toward Shea's."

That brought Leo's head up. "He was?"

Tess finished putting food on the table, so preoccupied by Cag's reappearance that she couldn't put two thoughts together in any sort of order. It was much harder to leave than she'd even anticipated.

She missed the comment about Shea's Bar entirely, and she barely touched her own food. She cleaned up the kitchen, blind to the brothers' troubled glances, and went to bed early. She felt like it was the end of the world.

So did Cag, who sat quietly at a corner table at Shea's Bar, drinking one whiskey highball after another until he was pleasantly numb and barely coherent.

No fool, he left the truck locked at the bar and took a cab back to the ranch. If the driver wondered at the identity of his overly-quiet passenger, he didn't ask. He took the bills that were fumbled out of the cowhide wallet and drove away.

Cag managed to get through the living room without falling over anything, amazing considering the amount of whiskey he'd imbibed. He made it to his own room and even into the shower, an undertaking of mammoth proportions.

With his hair still damp and only a short robe covering his nudity, it occurred to him that he should ask Tess why the rush to get away from the ranch. That it was three in the morning didn't seem to matter. If she was asleep, why she could just wake up and answer him.

He knocked at her door, but there was no answer. He opened it and walked in, bumping into a chair and the side table before he ever reached the bed.

He sat down on the side of it and noticed how hot the room was. She hadn't turned on the air conditioner, and then he remembered that his brothers had told him they'd shut the unit off temporarily while it was being worked on. No wonder it was so hot.

He reached out and pushed gently at Tess's shoulder

under the cover. She moaned and kicked the cover away and he caught his breath. She was lying there just in her briefs, without any other covering, her beautiful little breasts bare and firm in the muted light of the security lamp outside her window.

He couldn't help himself. He reached out and traced those pretty breasts with the tips of his fingers, smiling when she arched and they went hard-tipped at once.

It seemed the most natural thing in the world to slide out of his robe and into bed beside her.

He turned her against his nude body, feeling her quiver softly and then ease closer to him. She felt like heaven in his arms. The feel of her soft, warm skin so intimately kindled a raging arousal in him.

He moved her onto her back and slid over her, his mouth gently smoothing across her lips until they parted and responded despite the sharp tang of whiskey on his breath.

Half-asleep, and sure that she was dreaming, her arms went under his and around him, her legs moved to admit him into an intimacy that made his head spin. He moved against her blindly, hungrily, urgently, his mouth insistent on her mouth as he felt surges of pleasure breaking like waves inside him.

"Ca...Callaghan? Callaghan?" she whimpered.

"Yes, Tess...!" He caught her mouth again and his hand went to her thigh, pulling her even closer, straining against the thin nylon barrier that was all that separated them.

She didn't fight his seduction. If this was what he wanted, it was what she wanted, too. She relaxed and gave in to the sweet, fierce sensations that came from the intimate contact with his powerful body.

But even as his fingers sought her hips in a fierce urgency, the liquor finally caught up with him. He gave a soft, explosive sigh and a curse and suddenly went limp on her, the full weight of his body pressing her hard into the sheets.

She lay dazed, wondering exactly what had happened. Cag had no clothes on. She was wearing briefs, but nothing more. Not being totally stupid, she realized that sex involved a little more contact than this, but it was blatant intimacy, all the same. She shifted experimentally, but nothing happened. He'd been very aroused, but now he was relaxed all over.

She eased away a little and pushed. He went over onto his back in a liquid sprawl and with a long sigh.

Curious, she sat up in bed and looked at him, surprised at how much she enjoyed the sight of him like that. He might have been a warm statue for all the movement in him, but he was a delight even to her innocent eyes. She smiled secretively as she studied him unashamedly, thinking that for tonight he belonged to her, even if he didn't want to. After all, she hadn't coaxed him in here. He'd come of his own free will. He had to feel something for her, if he'd had to go out and get himself drunk to express what he really wanted.

While she looked at him she weighed her options. She could leave him here and shoo him out first thing in the morning—unless, of course, he awoke in the same condition he'd just been in except sober. In which case, her innocence was really going to be gone. Or she could try to get him back to his room. That would be impossible. He was deadweight. She could call the brothers to help her—but that would create a scandal.

In the end, she curled up beside him, pulled the sheet over both of them and went to sleep in his arms. Let tomorrow take care of itself, she mused while she enjoyed the feel of all that latent strength so close against her nudity. She loved him. If this was all she could ever have, she was going to have this one night. Even if he never knew about it.

Cag felt little hammers at either side of his head. He couldn't seem to open his eyes to discover what was the sound that had disturbed him. He remembered drinking a glass of bourbon whiskey. Several glasses. He remembered taking a shower and falling into bed. He remembered....

His eyes flew open and he sat straight up. But instead of looking at the bare back beside him, covered just decently by a sheet, he scanned his own nudity to the door, where Rey and Leo were standing frozen in place.

He jerked the sheet over his hips, held his throbbing head and said, predictably, "How did I get in here?"

"You bounder," Leo murmured, so delighted by his brother's predicament that he had to bite his tongue to keep from smiling. Finally he'd got Cag just where he wanted him!

"That goes double for me," Rey said, acting disgusted as he glanced toward Tess's prone figure barely covered by the sheet. "And she works for us!"

"Not anymore," Leo said with pure confidence as he folded his arms over his chest. "Guess who's getting married?" He raised his voice, despite Cag's outraged look. "Tess? Tess! Wake up!"

She forced her eyes open, glanced at Cag and froze. As she pulled up the sheet to her chin, she turned and saw the brothers standing poker-faced in the doorway.

Then she did what any sane woman might do under the circumstances. She screamed.

Chapter Ten

An awkward few minutes later, a cold sober and poleaxed Cag jerked into his robe and Tess retreated under the sheet until he left. He never looked at her, or spoke. She huddled into the sheet and wished she could disappear.

She felt terrible. Even though it wasn't her fault, any of it. She hadn't gone and climbed into bed with him, after all, and she certainly hadn't invited him into bed with her! When she'd dozed off, she'd been almost convinced that the whole episode had been a dream. Now it was more like a nightmare.

Tess went into the kitchen to make the breakfast that the brothers had found missing at its usual time. That was why they'd come looking for her, and how they knew Cag was in bed with her. She groaned as she realized what she was going to have to endure around the table. She decided beforehand that she'd eat her breakfast after they finished and keep busy in another part of the house until they were gone.

The meal was on the table when three subdued men walked into the kitchen and sat down. Tess couldn't look at any of them. She mumbled something about dusting the living room and escaped.

Not ten minutes later, Leo came looking for her.

She was cleaning a window that she'd done twice already. She couldn't meet his eyes.

"Was everything okay? I'm sorry if the bacon was a little overdone...."

"Nobody's blaming you for anything," he said, interrupting her quietly. "And Cag's going to do the right thing."

She turned, red-faced. "But he didn't do anything, Leo," she said huskily. "He was drunk and he got into the wrong bed, that's all. Nothing, absolutely nothing, went on!"

He held up a hand. "Cag doesn't know that nothing went on," he said, lowering his voice. "And you aren't going to tell him. Listen to me," he emphasized when she tried to interrupt, "you're the only thing that's going to save him from drying into dust and blowing away, Tess. He's alone and he's going to stay that way. He'll never get married voluntarily. This is the only way it will ever happen, and you know it."

She lifted her head proudly. "I won't trick him into marriage," she said curtly.

"I'm not asking you to. *We'll* trick him into it. You just go along."

"I won't," she said stubbornly. "He shouldn't have to marry me for something he didn't do!"

"Well, he remembers some of it. And he's afraid of what he can't remember, so he's willing to get married."

She was still staring at him with her eyes unblinking. "I love him!" she said miserably. "How can I ever expect him to forgive me if I let him marry me when he doesn't want to!''

"He does want to. At least, he wants to right now. Rey's gone for the license, you both go to the doctor in thirty minutes for a blood test and you get married Friday in the probate judge's office." He put a gentle hand on her shoulder. "Tess, if you love him, you have to save him from himself. He cares about you. It's so obvious to us that it's blatant. But he won't do anything about it. This is the only way he has a chance at happiness, and we're not letting him throw it away on half-baked fears of failure. So I'm sorry, but you're sort of the fall guy here. It's a gamble. But I'd bet on it.''

"What about when he remembers, if he does, and we're already married?" she asked plaintively.

"That's a bridge you can cross when you have to." He gave her a wicked grin. "Besides, you need an insurance policy against anything that might...happen."

"Nothing's going to happen!" she growled, her fists clenched at her side.

"That's what you think," he murmured under his breath, smiling—but only after he'd closed the door between them. He rubbed his hands together with gleeful satisfaction and went to find his sibling.

It was like lightning striking. Everything happened too fast for Tess's protests to make any differences. She wanted to tell Cag the truth, because she hadn't been drunk and she remembered what had gone on. But somehow she couldn't get him to herself for five minutes in the three days that followed. Before she knew what was happening, she and Cag were in the probate judge's office with Corrigan and Dorie, Simon and Tira, Leo and Rey behind them, cheering them on.

Tess was wearing a white off-the-shoulder cotton dress with a sprig of lily of the valley in her hair in lieu of a veil, and carrying a small nosegay of flowers. They were pronounced man and wife and Cag leaned down to kiss her—on the cheek, perfunctorily, even reluctantly. He looked more like a man facing an incurable illness than a happy bridegroom, and Tess felt more guilty by the minute.

They all went to a restaurant to have lunch, which Tess didn't taste. Afterward, Leo and Rey went on a hastily arranged business trip to California while Corrigan and Simon and their respective wives went to their own homes.

Cag put Tess into the Mercedes, which he drove for special occasions, and took her back to the ranch.

She wanted to tell him the truth, but the look on his face didn't invite confidences, and she was certain that it would only make things worse and get his brothers into big trouble if she confessed now.

She knew that nothing had happened that night, but if she slept with Cag, he was going to know it, too. Besides, sleeping with him would eliminate any ideas of an annulment. She'd been thinking about that all day, that she could give him his freedom before any more damage was done. She had to talk to him before tonight, before their wedding night.

It was almost time to put on dinner and she'd just started changing out of her wedding dress when the door opened and Cag came in, closing the door deliberately behind him.

In nothing but a bra and half-slip, she turned, brush in hand, to stare at him as if he were an apparition. He was wearing his jeans and nothing else. His broad chest was bare and there was a look in his black eyes that she didn't like.

"Cag, I have to tell you...."

Before she could get the rest of the sentence out, he had her up in his arms and he was kissing her. It wasn't like other kisses they'd shared, which had an affectionate, teasing quality to them even in passion. These were rough, insistent, arousing kisses that were a prelude to out-and-out seduction.

Tess didn't have the experience to save herself. A few feverish minutes later, she was twisting under him on the cover of the bed trying to help him get rid of the last little bit of fabric that concealed her from his eyes.

He was out of his jeans by then, and his mouth was all over her yielding body. He touched and tasted her in ways she'd never experienced, until she was writhing with hunger.

By the time he slid between her legs and began to possess her, she was so eager that the tiny flash of pain went almost unnoticed.

But not by Cag. He stopped at once when he felt the barrier give and lifted his head. His arms trembled slightly with the effort as he arched over her and put a rein on his desire long enough to search her wide, dazed eyes.

"I tried...to tell you," she stammered shakily when she realized why he was hesitating.

"If I could stop, I swear to God...I would!" he said in a hoarse, harsh whisper. He shuddered and bent to her mouth. "But it's too late! I'd rather die than stop!"

He kissed her hungrily as his body eased down and found a slow, sweet rhythm that brought gasps from the mouth he was invading. He felt her nails biting into his hips, pulling him, pleading, her whole body one long aching plea for satisfaction. She sobbed into his mouth as he gave her what she wanted in waves of sweet, hot ecstasy that built into a frightening crescendo just at the last.

She cried out and felt him shiver above her with the

same exquisite delight she was feeling. Seconds later, he collapsed in her arms and she took the weight of him with joy, clinging as he fought to get his breath. His heartbeat shook both of them in the damp, lazy aftermath.

She felt his breath at her ear, jerky and hot. "Did I hurt you?" he asked.

"No. Oh, no," she breathed, burrowing closer.

Her body moved just slightly and his own clenched. It had been years. He'd ached for Tess, for the fulfillment she'd just given him. It was too soon, and he wasn't going to get over this subterfuge that had made him her husband, but just now his mind wasn't the part of his body that was in control.

He moved experimentally and heard her breath catch even as sharp pleasure rippled up his spine. No, he thought as he pulled her under him again, it wasn't too soon. It wasn't too soon at all!

It was dark when he got out of bed and pulled his jeans back on. Tess was lying in a damp, limp, spent sprawl on the cover where he'd left her. She looked up at him with dazed blue eyes, her face rosy in the aftermath of passion, her body faintly marked where his hands and his mouth had explored her. She was his. She belonged to him. His head lifted with unconscious, arrogant pride of possession.

"How was it?" he asked.

She couldn't believe he'd said anything so blatant to her after the lovemaking that had been nothing short of a revelation. She hadn't dreamed that her body was capable of such sensations as she'd been feeling. And he asked her that question with the same interest he'd have shown about a weather report.

She stared at him, confused.

"Was it worth a sham wedding?" he continued, wounded by her silence that had made him feel obliged to go through with a wedding he didn't want. She'd trapped him and he felt like a fool, no matter how sweet the bait had been.

She drew the cover back over her nudity, ashamed because of the way he was looking at her. He made her feel as if she'd done something terrible.

"You knew nothing happened that night," he continued quietly. "I didn't. I was too drunk to care what I did, but I remembered all too well that I lost my head the minute I touched you. For all I knew, I might have gone through with it. But you knew better, and you let me marry you in spite of it, knowing it wasn't necessary."

She clutched the coverlet. "I tried to tell you, but I couldn't seem to get you alone for five minutes," she murmured defeatedly.

"Of course you couldn't," he returned. His voice was as cold as his eyes. "I wasn't going to make matters worse by seducing you a second time."

"I thought it was your brothers...."

She didn't finish, but her face gave the game away. His eyes positively glittered. "My brothers? Of course. My brothers!" He glared down at her. "They were in on it, too, weren't they? No wonder they did their best to make me feel like a heel! Did you convince them to go along with the lie?"

She wanted to tell him that it had been Leo's idea in the first place, but what good would it do now? He was making it clear that he'd married her against his will and blamed her for making it necessary. Nothing she could say would be much of a defense.

Her silence only made him madder. He turned toward the door.

"Where...are you going? Do you want supper?"

He looked at her over one broad, bare shoulder. "I've had all I want. Of everything."

He went through the doorway and slammed the door behind him.

Tess dissolved into tears of misery. Well, she was married, but at what cost? If Cag had ever been close to loving her, he wasn't anymore. He hated her; she'd seen it in his eyes. She'd trapped him and he hated her.

She got up, feeling unusually stiff and sore in odd places, and went to take a shower. The sooner she could get back to normal, or nearly normal, the better.

She bathed and dressed in a neat flowered shirtwaist dress, combed her freshly washed and dried curly hair and went to the kitchen to make supper. But even as she went into the room, she heard one of the ranch trucks crank up and roar away in a fury.

Curious, she searched the house for Cag, even braving his own bedroom. His closet was still open and she caught a whiff of aftershave. She leaned against the doorjamb with a long sigh. So he'd run out, on their wedding night. Well, what did she expect, that he'd stay home and play the part of the loving husband? Fat chance, after the things he'd said.

She fixed herself a sandwich with some cold roast beef and drank a glass of milk. Then she waited for Cag to come home.

When he hadn't come back by midnight, she went to her room and crawled into bed. She was certain that she laid awake for an hour, but she never heard him come in. She slept alone and miserable, still tingling with the memories of the past few hours. If only he'd loved her, just a little, she might have had hope. She had none, now.

By morning, she knew what she had to do. She went looking for Cag, to tell him she was leaving. She had the promise of her mother's legacy and a small savings account, plus last week's salary that she hadn't spent. She could afford a bus ticket and a cheap apartment somewhere, anywhere, out of Jacobsville.

It might have been just as well that Cag still hadn't come home. His room was empty, his bed hadn't been slept in. The brothers were still out of town and Mrs. Lewis wasn't coming again until the next week. Nobody would be here to say goodbye to her. But what did it matter? Cag had made his disgust and contempt very clear indeed. He wouldn't care if she left. She could get the divorce herself and have the papers sent to him. He didn't love her, so what reason was there to stay here and eat her heart out over a man who didn't want her?

She blushed a little as her mind provided vivid proof that it wasn't a case of his not wanting her physically. He'd been insatiable, inexhaustible. Perhaps that was why he left. Perhaps he was ashamed of how hungry he'd been for her, of letting her see that hunger. Her own inexperience had been her worst drawback, because she had no real knowledge of how men behaved after they'd soothed an ache. She didn't think a man in love would insult his new bride and leave her alone all night. Apparently he was still furious with her and in no mood to forgive what he saw as a betrayal of the worst kind.

Well, he needn't expect her to be sitting at home mourning his loss! She'd had enough of being alternately scorned, rejected and passionately kissed. He could find another object for his desires, like the noncooking Miss Brewster! And she wished the woman joy of him. Such a narrow-minded, hard-nosed man deserved a woman who'd lead him around by the ear!

Tess packed, took a long last look around the first real home she'd ever known and called a cab. She thought about leaving a note. But, after all, Cag hadn't left her one when he'd stayed out all night. He must have known that she'd be worried, but he hadn't cared about her feelings. Why should she care about his? Now it was her turn. But she was staying out much longer than a night.

She took the cab to the airport and walked into the terminal, staying only until the cab pulled away. She hailed another cab, climbed in and went to the bus station, just in case Cag tried to trace her. She wasn't going to make it easy for him! She bought a ticket for St. Louis and sat down to wait for the bus.

A plane ticket would have been nice, but she couldn't afford the luxury. She had to conserve her small store of cash. It would be enough to keep her for at least a week or two. After that, she could worry about getting enough to eat. But if she ran out of luck, there was always the shelter. Every city had one, full of compassionate people willing to help the down and out. If I ever get rich, she thought, I'll donate like crazy to keep those shelters open!

She *was* rich, she remembered suddenly, and bit her lip as she realized that she hadn't left the lawyer a forwarding address. She went to the nearest phone and, taking his card from her wallet, phoned and told his secretary that she was going out of town and would be in touch in a week or so. That business accomplished, she sat back down on one of the long benches and waited for the bus to arrive.

St. Louis was huge. Tess noticed barges going down the wide Mississippi and thought how much fun it would be to live in a river town. She'd lived inland all her life, it seemed.

She found a small efficiency apartment and paid a week's rent in advance. Then she bought a newspaper and got a sandwich from a nearby deli and went back to her room to read and eat.

There weren't a lot of jobs available. She could wait, of course, and hope for something she could do that paid a nice salary. But her skills were limited, and cooking was her best one. It seemed like kindly providence that there was a cooking job available at a local restaurant; and it was nearby!

She went the very next morning just after daylight to apply. The woman who interviewed her was dubious when Tess told her how old she was, but Tess promised she could do the job, which turned out to be that of a pastry chef.

The woman, still skeptical but desperate to fill the position, gave Tess a probationary job. Delighted, she got into the apron and cap and got started.

By the end of the day, her employer was quite impressed and Tess was hired unconditionally.

She went back to her apartment tired but satisfied that things had worked out for her so quickly. She spared a thought for Cag. If he'd come home, he probably wondered where she was. She didn't dare expand on that theme or she'd be in tears.

Running away had seemed the answer to all her problems yesterday, but it wasn't so cut-and-dried today. She was in a strange city where she had no family or friends, in a lonely apartment, and all she had to show for it was a job. She thought of the brothers waiting patiently for their breakfast and nobody there to fix it. She thought of Cag and how happy she'd felt that night she'd taken him the special dessert in his study. Things had been magical and for those few minutes, they'd belonged together. But how soon it had all fallen apart, through no real fault of her own.

"I should have stayed," she said, thinking aloud. "I should have made him listen."

But she hadn't. Now she had to live with the consequences. She hoped they wouldn't be too bad.

Callaghan dragged back into the house a day and a half after he'd left it with his misery so visible that it shocked his brothers, who'd come back from their business trip to an ominously empty house.

They surged forward when he walked through the door.

"Well?" Leo prompted impatiently, looking past Cag to the door. "Where is she?"

Cag's tired mind took a minute to work that question out. "Where is she? What do you mean, where is she? She isn't here?" he exploded.

Rey and Leo exchanged worried glances as Cag pushed past them and rushed down the hall to Tess's room. It was empty. Her suitcase was gone, her clothes were gone, her shoes were gone. He looked over her dresser and on the bed, but there was no note. She hadn't left a trace. Cag's heart turned over twice as he realized what she'd done. She'd run away. She'd left him.

His big fists clenched by his sides. His first thought was that he was glad she'd gone; his life could get back to normal. But his second thought was that he felt as if half his body was missing. He was empty inside. Cold. Alone, as he'd never been.

He heard his brothers come up behind him.

"Her things are gone," he said without any expression in his voice.

"No note?" Leo asked.

Cag shook his head.

"Surely she left a note," Rey murmured. "I'll check the office."

He went back down the hall. Leo leaned against the wall and stared unblinking at his big brother.

"Gave her hell, did you?" he asked pointedly.

Cag didn't look at him. His eyes were on the open closet door. "She lied. She tricked me into marriage." He turned his black eyes on Leo. "You helped her do it."

"Helped her? It was my idea," he said quietly. "You'd never have married her if it was left up to you. You'd have gone through life getting older and more alone, and Tess would have suffered for it. She loved you enough to risk it. I'd hoped you loved her enough to forgive it. Apparently I was wrong right down the line. I'm sorry. I never meant to cause this."

Cag was staring at him. "It was your idea, not hers?"

Leo shrugged. "She didn't want any part of it. She said if you didn't want to marry her, she wasn't going to do anything that would force you to. I talked her into keeping quiet and then Rey and I made sure you didn't have much time to talk to each other before the wedding." His eyes narrowed. "All of us care about you, God knows why, you're the blooming idiot of the family. A girl like that, a sweet, kind girl with no guile about her, wants to love you and you kick her out the door." He shook his head sadly. "I guess you and Herman belong together, like a pair of reptiles. I hope you'll be very happy."

He turned and went back down the hall to find Rey.

Cag wiped his forehead with his sleeve and stared blindly into space. Tess was self-sufficient, but she was young. And on top of all his other mistakes, he'd made one that caused the others to look like minor fumbles. He hadn't used anything during that long, sweet loving. Tess could be pregnant, and he didn't know where she was.

Chapter Eleven

Tess was enjoying her job. The owner gave her carte blanche to be creative, and she used it. Despite the aching hurt that Cag had dealt her, she took pride in her craft. She did a good job, didn't watch the clock and performed beautifully under pressure. By the end of the second week, they were already discussing giving her a raise.

She liked her success, but she wondered if Cag had worried about her. He was protective toward her, whatever his other feelings, and she was sorry she'd made things difficult for him. She really should call that lawyer and find out about her stock, so that she wouldn't have to depend on her job for all her necessities. And she could ask him to phone the brothers and tell them that she was okay. He'd never know where she was because she wasn't going to tell him.

She did telephone Clint Matherson, the lawyer, who was relieved to hear from her because he had, indeed, checked out those stocks her mother had left her.

"I don't know quite how to tell you this," he said heavily. "Your mother invested in a very dubious new company, which had poor management and little operating capital from the very start. The owner was apparently a friend of hers. To get to the point, the stock is worthless. Absolutely worthless. The company has just recently gone into receivership."

Tess let out a long breath and smiled wistfully. "Well, it was nice while it lasted, to think that she did remember me, that I was independently wealthy," she told the lawyer. "But I didn't count on it, if you see what I mean. I have a job as a pastry chef in a restaurant, and I'm doing very well. If you, uh, speak to the Hart brothers...."

"*Speak* to them!" he exclaimed. "How I'd love to have the chance! Callaghan Hart had me on the carpet for thirty minutes in my own office, and I never got one word out. He left his phone number, reminded me that his brother was acting attorney general of our state and left here certain that I'd call him if I had any news of you."

Her heart leaped into her throat. Callaghan was looking for her? She'd wondered if he cared enough. It could be hurt pride, that she'd walked out on him. It could be a lot of things, none of which concerned missing her because he loved her.

"Did you tell him about the stock?" she asked.

"As I said, Miss Brady, I never got the opportunity to speak."

"I see." She saw a lot, including the fact that the attorney didn't know she was married. Her spirits fell. If Callaghan hadn't even mentioned it, it must not matter to him. "Well, you can tell them that I'm okay. But I'm not telling you where I am, Mr. Matherson. So Callaghan can make a good guess."

"There are still papers to be signed..." he began.

"Then I'll find a way to let you send them to me, through someone else," she said, thinking up ways and means of concealing her whereabouts. "Thanks, Mr. Matherson. I'll get back to you."

She hung up, secure in her anonymity. It was a big country. He'd never find her.

Even as she was thinking those comforting thoughts, Clint Matherson was reading her telephone number, which he'd received automatically on his Caller ID box and copied down while they were speaking. He thought what a good thing it was that Miss Brady didn't know how to disable that function, if she even suspected that he had it. He didn't smirk, because intelligent, successful attorneys didn't do that. But he smiled.

Callaghan hadn't smiled for weeks. Leo and Rey walked wide around him, too, because he looked ready to deck anybody who set him off. The brothers had asked, just once, if Cag knew why Tess had left so abruptly and without leaving a note. They didn't dare ask again.

Even Mrs. Lewis was nervous. She was standing in for Tess as part-time cook as well as doing the heavy housework, but she was in awe of Callaghan in his black mood. She wasn't sure which scared her more, Cag or his scaly pet, she told Leo when Cag was out working on the ranch.

Always a hard worker, Cag had set new records for it since Tess's disappearance. He'd hired one private detective agency after another, with no results to date. A cabdriver with one of Jacobsville's two cab companies had been found who remembered taking her to the airport. But if she'd flown out of town, she'd done it under an assumed name and paid cash. It was impossible to find a clerk who remembered selling her a ticket.

Jacobsville had been thoroughly searched, too, but she wasn't here, or in nearby Victoria.

Callaghan could hardly tell his brothers the real reason that Tess had gone. His pride wouldn't let him. But he was bitterly sorry for the things he'd said to her, for the callous way he'd treated her. It had been a last-ditch stand to keep from giving in to the love and need that ate at him night and day. He wanted her more than he wanted his own life. He was willing to do anything to make amends. But Tess was gone and he couldn't find her. Some nights he thought he might go mad from the memories alone. She loved him, and he could treat her in such a way. It didn't bear thinking about. So he'd been maneuvered into marriage, so what? He loved her! Did it matter why they were married, if they could make it work?

But weeks passed with no word of her, and he had nightmares about the possibilities. She could have been kidnapped, murdered, raped, starving. Then he remembered her mother's legacy. She'd have that because surely she'd been in touch with…the lawyer! He could have kicked himself for not thinking of it sooner, but he'd been too upset to think straight.

Cag went to Matherson's office and made threats that would have taken the skin off a lesser man. She'd have to contact Matherson to get her inheritance. And when she did, he'd have her!

Sure enough, a few days after his visit there, the attorney phoned him.

He'd just come in from the stock pens, dirty and tired and worn to a nub.

"Hart," he said curtly as he answered the phone in his office.

"Matherson," came the reply. "I thought you might like to know that Miss Brady phoned me today."

Cag stood up, breathless, stiff with relief. "Yes? Where is she?"

"Well, I have Caller ID, so I got her number from the unit on my desk. But when I had the number checked out, it was a pay phone."

"Where?"

"In St. Louis, Missouri," came the reply. "And there's one other bit of helpful news. She's working as a pastry chef in a restaurant."

"I'll never forget you for this," Cag said with genuine gratitude. "And if you're ever in need of work, come see me. Good day, Mr. Matherson."

Cag picked up the phone and called the last detective agency he'd hired. By the end of the day, they had the name of the restaurant and the address of Tess's apartment.

Unwilling to wait for a flight out, Cag had a company Learjet pick him up at the Jacobsville airport and fly him straight to St. Louis.

It was the dinner hour by the time Cag checked into a hotel and changed into a nice suit. He had dinner at the restaurant where Tess worked and ordered biscuits.

The waiter gave him an odd look, but Cag refused to be swayed by offers of delicate pastries. The waiter gave in, shrugged and took the order.

"With apple butter," Cag added politely. He had experience enough of good restaurants to know that money could buy breakfast at odd hours if a wealthy customer wanted it and was willing to pay for the extra trouble.

The waiter relayed the order to Tess, who went pale and had to hold on to the counter for support.

"Describe the customer to me," she asked curtly.

The waiter, surprised, obliged her and saw the pale face go quite red with temper.

"He found me, did he? And now he thinks I'll cook him biscuits at this hour of the night!"

The assistant manager, hearing Tess's raised voice, came quickly over to hush her.

"The customer at table six wants biscuits and apple butter," the waiter said with resignation. "Miss Brady is unsettled."

"Table six?" The assistant manager frowned. "Yes, I saw him. He's dressed very expensively. If the man wants biscuits, bake him biscuits," he told Tess. "If he's influential, he could bring in more business."

Tess took off her chef's hat and put it on the counter. "Thank you for giving me the opportunity to work here, but I have to leave now. I make biscuits for breakfast. I don't make them for supper."

She turned and walked out the back door, to the astonishment of the staff.

The waiter was forced to relay the information to Cag, whose eyes twinkled.

"Well, in that case, I'll have to go and find her," he said, rising. "Nobody makes biscuits like Tess."

He left the man there, gaping, and went back to his hired car. With luck, he could beat Tess to her apartment.

And he did, with only seconds to spare as she got off the downtown bus and walked up the steps to her second-floor apartment.

Cag was standing there, leaning against the door. He looked worn and very tired, but his eyes weren't hostile at all. They were...strange.

He studied her closely, not missing the new lines in her face and the thinner contours of her body.

"You aren't cut out for restaurant work," he said quietly.

"Well, I'm not doing it anymore, thanks to you. I just

quit!'' she said belligerently, but her heart was racing madly at the sight of him. She'd missed him so badly that her eyes ached to look at him. But he'd hurt her. The wound was still fresh, and the sight of him rubbed salt in it. "Why are you here?" she continued curtly. "You said you'd had enough of me, didn't you?" she added, referring to what he'd said that hurt most.

He actually winced. "I said a lot of stupid things," he replied slowly. "I won't expect you to overlook them, and I'll apologize for every one, if you'll give me a chance to."

She seemed to droop. "Oh, what's the point, Callaghan?" she asked wearily. "I left. You've got what you wanted all along, a house without me in it. Why don't you go home?"

He sighed. He'd known it wouldn't be easy. He leaned his forearm against the wall and momentarily rested his head there while he tried to think of a single reason that would get Tess back on the ranch.

"Mrs. Lewis can't make biscuits," he said. He glanced at her. "We're all starving to death on what passes for her cooking. The roses are dying," he added, playing every card he had.

"It's been so dry," she murmured. Blue eyes met his. "Haven't you watered them?"

He made a rough sound. "I don't know anything about roses."

"But they'll die," she said, sounding plaintive. "Two of them are old roses. Antiques. They're precious, and not because of the cost."

"Wellll," he drawled, "if you want to save them, you better come home."

"Not with you there!" she said haughtily.

He smiled with pure self-condemnation. "I was afraid you'd feel that way."

"I don't want to come back."

"Too rich to bother with work that's beneath your new station?" he asked sarcastically, because he was losing and he couldn't bear to.

She grimaced. "Well, there isn't going to be any money, actually," she said. "The stocks are worthless. My mother made a bad investment and lost a million dollars." She laughed but it sounded hollow. "I'll always have to work for my living. But, then, I always expected to. I never really thought she'd leave anything to me. She hated me."

"Maybe she hated herself for having deserted you, did you think of that?" he asked gently. "She couldn't love you without having to face what she'd done, and live with it. Some people would rather be alone, than admit fault."

"Maybe," she said. "But what difference does it make now? She's dead. I'll never know what she felt."

"Would you like to know what I feel?" he asked in a different tone.

She searched his eyes coolly. "I already know. I'm much too young for you. Besides, I'm a weakness that you can't tolerate. And I lie," she added shortly. "You said so."

He stuck his hands deep into his pockets and stared at her with regret. "Leo told me the wedding was all his idea."

"Of course you'd believe your brother. You just wouldn't believe me."

His chest rose and fell. "Yes, that's how it was," he admitted, not bothering to lie about it. "I made you run away. Then I couldn't find you." His black eyes glittered. "You'll never know how that felt."

"Sure I know," she returned grimly. "It felt just the

same as when you walked out the door and didn't come back all night!''

He leaned against the wall wearily. He'd avoided the subject, walked around it, worried it to death. Now here it was. He lifted his gaze to her face. "I wanted you too badly to come home," he said. "I couldn't have kept my hands off you. So I spent the night in the bunkhouse."

"Gee, thanks for saving me," she muttered.

He stood erect with one of those lightning moves that once had intimidated her. "I should have come home and ravished you!" he said shortly. "At least you'd still be there now. You'd have been too weak to walk when I got through with you!"

She caught her breath. "Well!"

He moved forward and took her by the shoulders. He shook her gently. "Listen, redhead, I love you!" he said through his teeth, and never had a man looked less loverlike. "I want you, I need you and you're going home with me or I'll..."

Her breath was suspended somewhere south of her collarbone. "Or you'll what?" she asked.

He eased her back against the door and bent to her mouth. "Or you'll get what you escaped when I left you that night."

She lifted her mouth to his, relaxing under his weight as he pinned her there and kissed her so hungrily that she moaned. She clung to him. The past weeks had been so empty, so lonely. Cag was here, in her arms, saying that he loved her, and it wasn't a dream!

After a few feverish seconds, he forced himself to lift away from her.

"Let's go inside," he said in a tortured voice.

She only nodded. She fumbled her key into the lock and apparently he closed and locked it behind them. He didn't even turn on a light. He picked her up, purse and all, and carried her straight into the bedroom.

"Amazing how you found this room so easily when you've never been in here before," she whispered shakily as he laid her on the bed and began to remove everything that was in the way of his hands.

"Nesting instinct," he whispered, his hands urgent.

"Is that what it is?" She reached up, pushing at his jacket.

"First things first," he murmured, resisting her hands. When he had her out of her clothes, he started on his own.

Minutes later, he was beside her in the bed, but he did nothing about it, except to pull her completely against him and wrap her up under the covers.

"Oh, dear God," he groaned reverently as he held her close. "Tess, I was so afraid that I'd lost you! I couldn't have borne it."

She melted into him, aware of the stark arousal of his body. But he wasn't doing anything about it.

"I don't like being alone," she replied, nuzzling her face against his warm, bare chest.

"You won't be, ever again." His hands smoothed over her back. One eased between them to lie gently against her stomach. "How are you feeling?" he asked suddenly.

She knew what he was asking. "I don't think I'm pregnant," she answered the question he hadn't put into words. "I'm tired a lot, but that could be work stress."

"But you could be."

She smiled against him. If this was a dream, she hoped she didn't wake up too soon. "I guess so." She sighed. "Why? Nesting instinct?"

He chuckled. "Yes. I'm thirty-eight. I'd love kids. So would you. You could grow them along with your precious roses."

She stiffened. "My roses! Oh, Cag...!"

His intake of breath was audible. "That's the first time you've ever shortened my name."

"You didn't belong to me before," she said shyly.

His arms tightened. "And now I do?"

She hesitated. "I hope so."

"I know so. And you belong to me." He moved so that she was on her back. "I've been rough with you. Even the first time. Tonight, it's going to be so slow and silky sweet that you won't know your name by the time I've satisfied you." He bent and touched his mouth with exquisite tenderness to her parted lips.

"How conceited," she teased daringly.

He chuckled with a worldliness she couldn't match. "And we'll see about that...."

It was unexpectedly tender this time, a feast of exquisite touches and rhythms that progressed far too slowly for the heat he roused in her slim young body. She arched toward him and he retreated. He touched her and just as she trembled on the brink of ecstasy, he stopped touching her and calmed her. Then he started again.

On and on it went, so that time seemed to hang, suspended, around them. He taught her how to touch him, how to build the need and then deny it. She moaned with frustration, and he chuckled with pure joy.

When he heard her sob under the insistent pressure of his mouth, he gave in to the hunger. But even then, he resisted her clinging hands, her whispered pleadings.

"Make it last," he whispered at her open mouth, lazily moving against her. "Make it last as long as you can. When it happens, you'll understand why I won't let you be impatient."

She was shuddering already, throbbing. She met the

downward motion of his hips with upward movements of her own, her body one long plea for satisfaction.

"It's so...good," she whispered, her words pulsing with the rhythm of his body, the same throb in her voice that was in her limbs. "So good...!"

"It gets better," he breathed. He moved sinuously against her, a new movement that was so arousing that she cried out and clung to him with bruising fingers. "There?" he whispered. "Yes. There. And here...."

She was sobbing audibly. Her whole body ached. It was expanding, tense, fearsome, frightening. She was never going to live through it. She was blind, deaf, dumb, so much a part of him that she breathed only through him.

He felt her frantic motions, heard the shuddering desire in her voice as she begged him not to stop. He obliged her with smooth, quick, deep motions that were like stabs of pure pleasure. She closed her eyes and her teeth ground together as the tension suddenly built to unbearable heights and she arched up to him with her last ounce of strength.

"Yes. Now. Now, finally, now!" he said tightly.

There was no time. She went over some intangible edge and fell, throbbing with pleasure, burning with it, so oblivious to her surroundings that she had no idea where she was. She felt the urge deep in her body, growing, swelling, exploding. At some level she was aware of a harsh groan from the man above her, of the fierce convulsion of his body that mirrored what was happening to hers.

She lost consciousness for a few precious seconds of unbearable pleasure, and then sobbed fiercely as she lost it even as it began.

He held her, comforted her. His mouth touched her eyes, her cheeks, her open mouth. Her body was still locked closely into his, and when she was able to open her eyes, she saw his pupils dilated, glittering with the remnants of passion.

"Do you know that I love you, after that," he whispered unsteadily, "or would you like to hear it a few dozen more times?"

She managed to shake her head. "I...felt it," she whispered back, and blushed as she realized just how close they were. "I love you, too. But you knew that already."

"Yes," he replied tenderly, brushing back her damp, curly hair. "I knew it the first time you let me touch you." He smiled softly at her surprise. "You were so very innocent, Tess. Not at all the sort of girl who'd permit liberties like that to just any man. It had to be love for you."

"It wasn't for you," she said quietly. "Not at first."

"Oh, yes, it was," he denied. His fingers lingered near her ear. "I started fighting you the day you walked into the kitchen. I wanted you so badly that I ached every time I looked at you." He smiled ruefully. "I was so afraid that you'd realize it."

"Why didn't you say so?" she asked.

His fingers contracted. "Because of the bad experience I had with a younger woman who threw me over because she thought I was too old for her." His shoulders moved. "You were even younger than she was at the time." His eyes were dark, concerned. "I was in over my head almost at once, and I thought I'd never be enough for you..."

"Are you nuts?" she gasped. "Enough for me? You're too *much* for me, most of the time! I can't match you. Especially like this. I don't know anything!"

"You're learning fast," he mused, looking down their joined bodies in the light from the night-light. "And you love like a poem," he whispered. "I love the way you feel in my arms like this. You make me feel like the best lover in the world."

"You are," she said shyly.

"Oh, no," he argued. "It's only because you don't have anyone to compare me with."

"It wouldn't matter," she said.

He touched her cheek gently. "I don't guess it would," he said then. "Because it's like the first time, every time I'm with you. I can't remember other women."

She hit him. "You'd better not!"

He grinned. "Love me?"

She pressed close. "Desperately."

"Try to get away again," he invited. "You're my wife. You'll never get past the first fence."

She traced a path on his shoulder and frowned. "I just thought of something. Where are your brothers?"

"Leo and Rey are in Denver."

"What are they doing in Denver?" she asked.

He sighed. "Getting away from me. I've been sort of hard to get along with."

"You don't say! And that's unusual?"

He pinched her lightly, making her squeal. "I'll be a model of courtesy starting the minute we get home. I promise."

Her arms curled around his neck. "When are we going home?"

He chuckled and moved closer, sensuous movements that began to have noticeable results. "Not right now...."

It was two days later when they got back to the Hart ranch. And they still hadn't stopped smiling.

Tess had decided not to pursue her horticulture education just yet, because she couldn't leave Cag when she'd only just really found him. That could wait. So she had only one last tiny worry, about sleeping in the same room with an escaping Herman, although she loved Cag more than enough to tolerate his pet—in another bedroom.

But when she opened the door to Cag's room, which she would now share, the big aquarium was gone. She turned to Cag with a worried expression.

He put his arms around her and drew her close, glad that his brothers and Mrs. Lewis hadn't arrived just yet.

"Listen," he said softly, "remember that nesting instinct I told you I had?"

She nodded.

"Well, even the nicest birds don't keep a snake in the nest, where the babies are," he said, and his whole face smiled tenderly as he said it.

She caught her breath. "But you love him!"

"I love you more," he said simply. "I gave him to a friend of mine, who, coincidentally, has a female albino python. Speaking from experience, I can tell you that deep down any bachelor is far happier with a female of his own species than with any pet, no matter how cherished it is."

She touched his cheek lovingly. "Thank you."

He shrugged and smiled down at her. "I built the nest," he reminded her. "Now it's your turn."

"Want me to fill it, huh?"

He grinned.

She hugged him close and smiled against his broad chest. "I'll do my very best." Her heart felt full unto bursting. "Cag, I'm so happy."

"So am I, sweetheart." He bent and kissed her gently. "And now, there's just one more thing I need to make me the most contented man on earth."

She looked up at him expectantly, with a wicked gleam in her blue eyes. "Is there? What is it?" she asked suggestively.

"A pan of biscuits!" he burst out. "A great, big pan of biscuits! With apple butter!"

"You fraud! You charlatan! Luring me back here because of your stomach instead of your...Cag!"

He was laughing like a devil as he picked her up and tossed her gently onto the bed.

"I never said I wouldn't sing for my supper," he murmured dryly, and his hands went to his shirt buttons as he stood over her.

She felt breathless, joyful, absolutely gloriously loved. "In that case," she whispered, "you can have *two* pansful!"

By the time the brothers arrived that evening, Cag had already gone through half a panful. However, he seemed more interested in Tess than the food, anyway, so the brothers finally got their fill of biscuits after a long, dry spell.

"What are you two going to do when I build Tess a house like Dorie's got?" Cag asked them.

They looked horrified. Just horrified.

Rey put down his half-eaten biscuit and stared at Leo. "Doesn't that just beat all? Every time we find a good biscuit-maker, somebody goes and marries her and takes her away! First Corrigan, now him!"

"Well, they had good taste, you have to admit," Leo continued. "Besides, Tira can't bake at all, and Simon married her!"

"Simon isn't all that crazy about biscuits."

"Well, you do have a point there," Leo conceded.

Rey stared at Tess, who was sitting blatantly on her husband's lap feeding him a biscuit. He sighed. He'd been alone a long time, too.

"I'm not marrying anybody to get a biscuit," he said doggedly.

"Me, neither," Leo agreed, stuffing another one into his mouth. "Tell you what—" he pointed his apple butter spoon at Rey "—he can put up his house in the daytime and we'll take it down at night."

"You can try," Cag said good-naturedly.

"With our luck, we'll never find wives. Or if we do," Leo added dolefully, "they won't be able to cook at all."

"This is a great time to find a veteran housekeeper who can make bread," Cag stated. "Somebody who can take care of both of you when we move out."

"I can take care of myself," Rey muttered.

"So can I," Leo agreed.

"Be stubborn," Cag said. "But you'll change your tune one day."

"In a pig's eye!" they both said at once.

Later, lying in Tess's soft arms, Cag remembered when he'd said the same things his brothers just had.

"They'll fall like kingpins one day," he told Tess as he smoothed her hair.

"If they're lucky," she agreed.

He looked down into her gentle eyes and he wasn't smiling. "If they're very lucky," he whispered. "Was I worth all the trouble, Tess?"

She nodded. "Was I?"

"You were never any trouble." He kissed her tenderly. "I'm sorry I gave you such a hard time."

"You're making up for it," she returned, pulling him down to her. "I'd rather have you than that million dollars, Cag," she breathed into his lips. "I'd rather have you than the whole world!"

If Cag hadn't been so busy following his newly acquired nesting instinct, he could have told her the same thing. But he was certain that she knew it already.

* * * * *

Coming in May from Steeple Hill Books....

BLIND PROMISES

by bestselling author

Diana Palmer

(originally published under the pseudonym Katy Currie)

makes a long-awaited return in Love Inspired
with this tender, heartstirring story about the
healing power of love.

Just turn the page for an exciting preview....

Dana Steele paid the taxi driver and went up the cobblestone path to the door, pausing before she rang the doorbell. The house was fairly large, built of gray stone and overlooking the Atlantic, so ethereal that it might have been an illusion. Dana loved it at first sight. It's beautiful, she thought, with flowers blooming all around it and the greenery profuse.

Well, she told herself, it was now or never. Subconsciously she tugged a lock of her loosened hair over her cheek to help conceal the scar. Bangs already hid the one on her forehead. But the worst scars were those inside, out of sight.

The door opened and a small dark woman with green eyes stood smiling at her.

"You're Dana Steele?" she asked softly. "Come in. I'm Lorraine van der Vere and am so glad to meet you."

Dana compared her own gray suit with the woman's obviously expensive emerald pantsuit and felt shabby in comparison. It was the best she had, of course, but hardly couture. If what Mrs. van der Vere was wearing was any indication, the family was quite wealthy.

"Would you like to go upstairs and freshen up before I, uh, introduce you to my son?"

Dana was about to reply when there was a crash and a thud, followed by muffled words in a deep, harsh voice. Probably a servant had dropped something in the kitchen, Dana thought, but Mrs. van der Vere looked suddenly uncomfortable.

"Dana, if I may call you Dana, you're used to difficult patients, aren't you?" she asked.

Dana smiled. "Yes, Mrs. van der Vere."

"Call me Lorraine, dear. We're going to be allies, you know." She straightened. "Shall we get it over with?"

Dana followed behind her, half-puzzled. Surely, the little Dutch gentleman couldn't be that much of a horror. She wondered if he'd have an accent. His mother didn't seem to...

Lorraine knocked tentatively on the door of the room next to the living room.

"Gannon?" she called hesitantly.

"Well, come in or go away! Do you need an engraved invitation?" came a deep, lightly accented voice from behind the huge mahogany door.

Lorraine opened the door and stood aside to let Dana enter the room first. "Here's your new nurse, darling. Miss Dana Steele. Dana, this is my stepson, Gannon."

Dana barely heard her. She was trying to adjust to the fact that the small, mustached Dutch gentleman she had been told was to be her patient was actually the man she saw in front of her.

"Well?" the huge man at the desk asked harshly, his unseeing gray eyes staring straight ahead. "Is she mute, Mother? Or just weighing the advantages of silence."

Dana found her voice and moved forward, her footsteps alerting the tall blond man to her approach. He stood up, towering over her, his shaggy mane of hair falling roguishly over his broad forehead.

"How do you do, Mr. van der Vere?" Dana asked with more confidence than she felt.

"I'm blind—how do you think I do, Miss Steele?" he demanded harshly, his deep voice cold and cutting, his wintery eyes glaring at her. "I trip over furniture. I turn over glasses, and I hate being led around like a child! Did my stepmother tell you that you're the fifth?" he added with a bitter laugh.

"Fifth what?" she asked, holding on to her nerve.

"Nurse, of course," he replied impatiently. "I've gone through that many in a month. How long do you expect to last?"

"As long as I need to, Mr. van der Vere," she replied calmly.

He cocked his head, as if straining to hear her. "Not afraid of me, miss?" he prodded.

She shifted her shoulders. "Actually, sir, I'm quite fond of wild animals," she said with a straight face, while Lorraine gaped at her.

A faint movement in the broad face caught her attention. "Are you presuming to call me a wild animal?" he retorted.

"Oh, no, sir," Dana assured him. "I wouldn't flatter you on such short acquaintance."

He threw back his head and laughed. "Nervy, aren't you?" he murmured. "You'll need that nerve if you stay here long." He turned away and found the corner of the desk, easing himself back into his chair.

"Well, I'll leave you two to…get acquainted," Lorraine

said, seizing her opportunity. She backed out the door with an apologetic smile at Dana, and closed it behind her.

"Would you like to get acquainted with me, Miss Nurse?" Gannon van der Vere asked arrogantly.

"Oh, definitely, sir. I do consider it an advantage to get to know the enemy."

He chuckled. "Is that how you see me?"

"That's obviously how you want to be seen," she told him. "You don't like being nursed, do you? You'd rather sit behind that great desk and brood about being blind."

The smile faded and his eyes glittered sightlessly toward the source of her voice. "I beg your pardon?"

"Have you been out of this house since the accident?" she asked. "Have you bothered to learn braille, or to walk with a cane? Have you seen about getting a seeing-eye dog?"

"I don't need crutches!" he shot back. "I'm a man, not a child. I won't be fussed over!"

"But you must see that the only recourse you've given your stepmother is to find help for you…" she said, attempting reason. "…if you won't even make the effort to help yourself."

He lifted his nose in what Dana immediately recognized as the prelude to an outburst of pure venom.

"Perhaps I would if I could be left alone long enough," he replied in a voice so cold it dripped icicles. "I've been 'helped' out of my mind. The last nurse my stepmother brought here had the audacity to suggest that I might benefit from a psychiatrist. She left in the middle of the night."

"I can see you now, flinging her out the front steps in her bathrobe," Dana retorted, unperturbed.

"Impertinent little creature, aren't you?" he growled.

"If you treat your employees this way, Mr. van der

Vere, I'm amazed that you still have any," she said calmly. "Now, what would you like for dinner and I'll show you how to start feeding yourself. I assume you don't like being spoon-fed?"

He muttered something harsh and banged his fist down on the desk. "I'm not hungry!"

"In that case I'll tell the cook not to bother preparing anything for you," she said cheerfully. "When you do need me, call."

She started out the door, trying not to hear what he was saying to her back. She reminded him sweetly, "Sticks and stones, Mr. van der Vere..."

In August, Diana Palmer introduces three more legendary heroes in her brand-new Silhouette short story collection—
LOVE WITH A LONG, TALL TEXAN.
Don't miss these three irresistible tales of love, passion and heart-stopping adventure!

Silhouette ROMANCE™

In March,
award-winning,
bestselling author
Diana Palmer joins
Silhouette Romance in
celebrating the one year
anniversary of its
successful promotion:

VIRGIN BRIDES

*Celebrate the joys of
first love with unforgettable
stories by our most beloved authors....*

**March 1999:
CALLAGHAN'S BRIDE
Diana Palmer**

Callaghan Hart exasperated temporary ranch cook
Tess Brady by refusing to admit that the attraction they
shared was more than just passion. Could Tess make
Callaghan see she was his truelove bride before her time
on the Hart ranch ran out?

Silhouette®

Available at your favorite retail outlet.

If you enjoyed what you just read,
then we've got an offer you can't resist!

Take 2 bestselling love stories FREE!
Plus get a FREE surprise gift!

Clip this page and mail it to Silhouette Reader Service™

IN U.S.A.	IN CANADA
3010 Walden Ave.	P.O. Box 609
P.O. Box 1867	Fort Erie, Ontario
Buffalo, N.Y. 14240-1867	L2A 5X3

YES! Please send me 2 free Silhouette Romance® novels and my free surprise gift. Then send me 6 brand-new novels every month, which I will receive months before they're available in stores. In the U.S.A., bill me at the bargain price of $2.90 plus 25¢ delivery per book and applicable sales tax, if any*. In Canada, bill me at the bargain price of $3.25 plus 25¢ delivery per book and applicable taxes**. That's the complete price and a savings of over 10% off the cover prices—what a great deal! I understand that accepting the 2 free books and gift places me under no obligation ever to buy any books. I can always return a shipment and cancel at any time. Even if I never buy another book from Silhouette, the 2 free books and gift are mine to keep forever. So why not take us up on our invitation. You'll be glad you did!

215 SEN CNE7
315 SEN CNE9

Name		(PLEASE PRINT)	
Address		Apt.#	
City		State/Prov.	Zip/Postal Code

* Terms and prices subject to change without notice. Sales tax applicable in N.Y.
** Canadian residents will be charged applicable provincial taxes and GST.
   All orders subject to approval. Offer limited to one per household.
   ® are registered trademarks of Harlequin Enterprises Limited.

SROM99   ©1998 Harlequin Enterprises Limited

This March Silhouette is proud to present

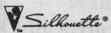 **Silhouette®**

SENSATIONAL

MAGGIE SHAYNE
BARBARA BOSWELL
SUSAN MALLERY
MARIE FERRARELLA

This is a special collection of four complete
novels for one low price, featuring a novel
from each line: Silhouette Intimate Moments,
Silhouette Desire, Silhouette Special Edition
and Silhouette Romance.

Available at your favorite retail outlet.

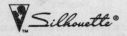

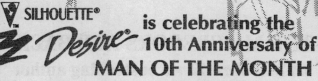
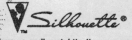

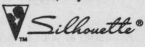

THESE BACHELOR DADS NEED A LITTLE TENDERNESS—AND A WHOLE LOT OF LOVING!

January 1999—A Rugged Ranchin' Dad
by Kia Cochrane (SR# 1343)
Tragedy had wedged Stone Tyler's family apart. Now this rugged rancher would do everything in his power to be the perfect daddy—and recapture his wife's heart—before time ran out....

April 1999 —Prince Charming's Return
by Myrna Mackenzie (SR# 1361)
Gray Alexander was back in town—and had just met the son he had never known he had. Now he wanted to make Cassie Pratt pay for her deception eleven years ago...even if the price was marriage!

And in June 1999 don't miss Donna Clayton's touching story of Dylan Minster, a man who has been raising his daughter all alone.....

Fall in love with our FABULOUS FATHERS!

And look for more FABULOUS FATHERS in the months to come. Only from

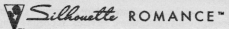

Silhouette ROMANCE™

Available wherever Silhouette books are sold.

Look us up on-line at: http://www.romance.net

SRFFJ-J

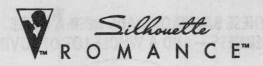

COMING NEXT MONTH